Praise for Jon Bilbao

"A tense and intense novel that culminates in outlandish violence. The narrative unfolds almost cinematically—think Quentin Tarantino with a dash of *Key Largo* and *Touch of Evil* . . . A terrific, anxious, and disturbing read."—*Kirkus Reviews* (**Starred review**)

"An invigorating challenge. The reader indeed finds in [*Still the Same Man*] entertainment, emotions and intrigue, but also reflection and thought on grave issues."—**Lluís Satorras,** *Babelia*

To speak of Jon Bilbao is to speak of one of the most important figures in Spanish narrative of the twenty-first century and, in particular, of the short distances of the story."—**Marcos Gendre,** *Mondo Sonoro*

"Mixing the everyday with the extraordinary doesn't always work, but Jon Bilbao manages to do it without having to write 400 pages . . ."—**Pilar Martin,** *Hola News*

". . . Bilbao dominates like few others in Spanish letters."—**Paula Corroto,** *El Confidencial*

Jon Bilbao

THE STRANGERS

Translated by Katie Whittemore

DALKEY ARCHIVE PRESS

Dallas / Dublin

Originally published in Spanish as *Los extraños* by Impedimenta
Copyright © 2021 by Jon Bilbao
Translation copyright © 2023 by Katie Whittemore
First edition
Paperback: 978-1-62897-455-3
Ebook: 978-1-62897-482-9
Library of Congress Cataloging-in-Publication Data: Available.

Cover design by Nuno Moreira
Interior design by Anuj Mathur

www.dalkeyarchive.com
Dallas / Dublin

Printed on permanent/durable acid-free paper.

PART I

KATHARINA HEARS HIM TYPING in the living room. She's in their shared bedroom, the most spacious room in the house, where he slept as a child. If she wanted to speak to him in person, she would have to cross the big bedroom, proceed down an eight-meter long hallway, descend a set of fifteen stairs, turn left on the lower landing, and knock on the leaded glass door leading to the downstairs living room. Yet she can still hear him typing on his computer. Very few cars drive by on the road out front. Whenever one breaks the silence, the swish of tires on the wet asphalt makes her even more depressed. It's been raining nonstop for four days. Lying in bed, propped up by a damp-smelling pillow, laptop on her knees, she wastes time online instead of working. She opens a chat window to communicate with Jon.

What are you doing?

He's slow to reply. He must be wrapping up a paragraph.

Ocean ridges.

They're assigning him geology topics now. Before, it was thermal machinery. Before that, physics.

Tea?

Again, a delayed response.

Later. But you have some.

She doesn't insist. It's Friday; she knows he wants to finish his weekly quota of chapters and send them off.

It's been a while since Katharina heard any sound from the kitchen. Lorena, the woman who cleans and makes their meals, must be taking one of her naps. She's worked for Jon's family for years. She keeps an armchair, a radio, and magazines in the pantry room and, on one of the cupboard shelves, in front of the jars of olives and cans of tuna, framed photos of her grandchildren beside a picture of Our Lady of Covadonga.

She wants a cup of tea but doesn't feel like seeing Lorena. Outside the window, a cypress grows taller than the house, blocking the view almost entirely. Through the drizzle, the estuary is just visible on either side of the tree, and on the other bank, the town. The church bell tolls. Five.

She's translating an orthodontics manual into German. The text has six authors: two Mexicans, two Colombians, a Peruvian, and an Argentinean; each uses expressions and turns of phrase typical of the Spanish spoken in his or her country; none of them write well. Jon said he would help her when she accepted the job. He hasn't. He gave her a little stand to hold the book open beside the computer, that's it. Katharina keeps the file open, but she hasn't translated anything today. Like he does every evening, Jon will ask her how many pages she's gotten through. She is irritated ahead of time.

The church bell tolls. Five-thirty.

She's startled by her phone. She looks at the screen. Her father. She knows very well what he wants to say, and she also knows that—if she hears it one more time—it's very possible she'll give in. She rejects the call.

The church bell tolls. Six.

She relaxes a bit. This is when he usually stops working and Lorena goes home. Nonetheless, she can still hear the distant click of the keys in the living room. She peeks into the hallway. By now she knows which floorboards creak the loudest. On her way to the bathroom, she steps heavily on each one of them. She flushes the toilet. Shuts the door firmly. On her way back to the bedroom, she jumps from floorboard to floorboard on one foot, as if playing hopscotch.

The church bell tolls. Six-thirty.

"I'm going now!"

Katharina starts. Now she's the one who's nodded off.

"I left food!"

Lorena shouts from the hallway, at the top of the stairs leading to the lower level.

Jon, from the living room: Thanks, Lorena! See you Monday!

Katharina waits until she hears the door close.

Then she waits a little longer, in case Lorena has

forgotten something and comes back inside. This happens often. Sometimes she's stealthy about it, armed with some ridiculous excuse—grabbing a pack of tissues or closing a window she left half-open—as if she was hoping to catch them engaged in intimate or offensive behavior. When she hears Lorena's moped backfire, Katharina goes into the kitchen and lifts the lid on the casserole dish cooling on the stovetop. Stewed beef with artichokes and peas, just like last weekend. According to Lorena, stewed beef "holds up well." In the fridge, plastic containers and tinfoil-wrapped plates with the entire week's leftovers. She sniffs them one by one and tosses the contents into the trash.

I'm going to the grocery store.
Want help?
No.

She puts on her raincoat and heads outside. It's already April. When she complains about the bad weather, Jon replies that the days are longer, at least. Katharina is of the opinion that this simply prolongs the grayness. The back door opens onto the steep hillside on which the house is built. Sheltering under the eaves, she inhales the scent of sodden earth and vegetation. She rounds the house and takes a few stone steps down to the detached garage. From there, a slippery cobbled driveway runs down to the entrance to the property at street level. Before reaching the metal-grille gate, there is a cave, an old natural outflow for the hill. Since Katharina doesn't know how to reverse down the steep drive, that's where they park the car.

Although there's a better-stocked supermarket on the outskirts of Ribadesella, Katharina likes to shop in the small stores in town, where she sees more people and can exchange a few words with the shop-keepers. She wants to fix a casual supper. She believes she deserves this indulgence. She buys olive pâté, salmon, clams, and a bottle of white wine. She fin-ishes the shopping sooner than she would like. She wishes she could pop into a bar, order a beer, chat with somebody, but Jon doesn't have any friends in town. He left a long time ago. He has acquaintances, but no one he wants to hang out with, and thus she is deprived of a social life.

She gets back in the car and crosses the bridge that spans the estuary. Then, instead of turning left toward home, she drives on in the direction of the beach. She'll take a little walk, delay her return, despite the rain.

The estuary curves around the base of Monte Corbero and discharges into the sea at one end of the beach. It courses, piquant, after all the rain. The beach looks very different from the image it projects in the summer, when she and Jon typically come to spend a few days and his parents are home and take care of everything and insist that Katharina and Jon go have a swim and relax as much as they can. Now, dark bands of marine litter and plastic debris cut across the sand. Jon's parents winter in the Canary Islands.

Three youths outfitted in waterproof gear have built a bonfire with driftwood. The wood is wet and it's still drizzling; they have to feed the fire with lighter fluid from a tin container. While one kid tends to the blaze, the others sift through the litter, looking for spray cans. When they find one, they throw it onto the flames, retreat, and wait, bouncing on their toes until the heat ignites whatever is left in the can and launches it like a missile. If it whizzes by close to one, they put their hands on their heads and howl. They're accompanied by a Rottweiler busy destroying an empty bleach bottle. With every explosion, the dog shrinks and glances around in fear.

Leaning with her elbows on the railing that runs alongside the beach, the hood of her raincoat up, Katharina watches the boys until one notices and returns her stare. Katharina sniffs hard through her nose. She's getting a cold. The boy lifts his chin; it could be a greeting or an invitation to get lost. Katharina clears her throat and spits the phlegm into the sand.

Back yet?

At the beach. Came for a walk.

How is it?

Loud.

Loud?

The waves, the wind. I don't know.

During dinner, she keeps refilling Jon's wine glass. "You trying to get me drunk?"

"Absolutely."

They leave the dishes on the table and move to the upstairs sitting room, which is smaller than the downstairs living room but cozier, too. Jon brings his glass of wine.

"Movie?" Katharina asks. Not waiting for his answer, she goes to get her laptop.

She returns to the sitting room, types in a porn site, and chooses a video: a girl with two men. She sets the laptop on the coffee table and settles in beside Jon. Katharina isn't really into porn; she considers it a last resort. She takes a sip from Jon's glass. There's no lead-in to the video; no one has bothered to set the scene or create expectations. It kicks right off with a man on either side of the girl, touching her. The men are naked. The set is a Finnish sauna, but the girl is dressed in lingerie and heels. She abides them, gripping their cocks like she's clinging to a set of handlebars. Katharina touches Jon's groin. The video's pacing is too slow, the shots too long, and none of the actors are attractive.

"Should we put on a different one?" Katharina suggests, and Jon nods. "Do you want to choose?"

"No, pick something you like."

The second video is extremely low-res and the third—staged in a prison—is of such poor quality that eventually Katharina gets frustrated and proposes they turn it off. Porn isn't doing the trick anyway. They lack the appetite. Or they're never in the mood at the same time. They discuss it again. They congratulate themselves on their ability to be rational and assure each other there is no cause for concern. It will pass. They attribute it to the situation. They kiss and embrace.

"Want to watch a real movie?" Jon says.

Katharina doesn't answer. She stares in alarm over at the window, which looks out over the estuary and the town.

"What's that?"

They stand. He stumbles into the coffee table, almost knocking the laptop onto the floor.

"I can't tell," he says. "Turn off the light."

Katharina obeys.

Lights. In the sky over the town. Unlike a plane's navigation lights, they aren't blinking. The lights belong to three objects and define the shape of each one: triangular, circular, and oblong. Red, green, and blue respectively. It's impossible to judge the size of the objects, or how far away they are. They aren't moving at first. For several moments they remain motionless, before they start to glide—alternating, zigzagging in the sky, as if performing a sort of choreography, or chess moves on an invisible board. Possibly an effect of the fine rain still falling, their movements leave a trace of light blue in their wake, as if the objects had wiped away a swath of night and allowed a fleeting glimpse of daytime sky. The three shapes then begin to move in unison; the circular and oblong objects chase the triangle, which evades them, smaller, speedier, swerving and dodging to get away. This game or maneuver lasts but seconds, after which the objects reconvene and fly off over Monte Corbero together, in the direction of the sea, and disappear out of sight.

Pressed to the window, Katharina and Jon wait in silence for something else to happen, for the objects to return or some sort of response to occur. On the other side of the estuary, the town appears unfazed. No more house lights on than before, no fewer. No extra cars out on the bridge or on any of the streets they can see. Jon opens the window to check if they can hear something: anxious voices, sirens. Nothing.

"It's cold," she says. "Close the window, please."

Katharina switches on the lamp. Now that the lights in the sky have vanished, the gloom in the sitting room is unbearable.

Once Katharina is asleep, Jon gets out of bed. He feels around on the chair where he leaves his clothes and pulls a thick sweater on over his pajamas. He avoids the creaky boards in the hall. He enters the sitting room. The first thing he does is look out the window. The only change is that the rain has stopped. The sky is calm. He picks up Katharina's phone, left on the coffee table next to the laptop. He unlocks the screen and checks her call history. He heard someone ring her this afternoon while he was working. Her father. Urging her to come back to Munich, surely. That she rejected the call does little to soothe him. He goes through her messages and emails. Almost all of it is in German, a language he knows very little of. There are a few emails in English, all from audiovisual production companies: none of them need anyone at the moment, but they'll keep her resume on file.

In a notebook, at the kitchen table, he records what he saw in the sky. Writing it down prolongs the experience. At the same time, it tempers the effect the lights have produced in him, an effect that keeps him awake. He is even more excited than when Katharina told him she was pregnant. It happened right after they got settled in at the house. It wasn't planned.

Out of the corner of his eye, he sees a flash in the sky. He runs to the sitting room, where the view is better. A helicopter is circling over the town. A short time later, it too heads toward the sea, following the route the objects took. Before bed, he and Katharina had turned on the radio. They spent a long time discussing what they'd seen in the sky. There had still been no visible changes to the town. The local radio station concluded the broadcast of the news at midnight with the mention of some strange lights seen over Ribadesella. That was it. A few newspapers published photos online, sent in by witnesses. The images, all of them, were disappointing: the night sky and a few colored dots, insignificant, trivial, easily confused with a reflection from the lens. None of the photos did justice to what Jon and Katharina had witnessed: something unprecedented, briefly superimposed on reality; something, he thought, that Katharina might interpret as the sign to leave she's been waiting for.

***

It's not raining in the morning. In some places, the clouds have even parted. Jon suggests they walk into town for coffee and to see what people are saying about the lights. At the bottom of the driveway, a couple is standing on the other side of the gate. They appear to be arguing in low voices. The man points insistently up at the house. Each is carrying a bulky suitcase. The girl spots Katharina and Jon and motions for her companion to be quiet.

"Hello," the man says, waving and grinning. "Jon?"

"Yeah."

"Glad to see you, cousin."

They appear to be the same ages as Jon and Katharina—the man, in his mid-thirties; the woman, a few years younger—but they're in better shape. They're very tan. He's wearing a bomber jacket and chinos. The northeasterly breeze ruffles his abundant blond hair; some streaks so light they look white, reflecting the feeble sunlight. One look is enough to know he spends a lot of time doing his hair, then undoing it just enough. He has a wide, easy smile. He's reminiscent of Robert Redford, but with a Basque nose. She has long, slender legs. In heels, she's taller than he is. She's wearing a fur coat and sunglasses. Her hair falls to her waist, straight and inky black.

Jon, suspicious, approaches the gate.

"I'm Markel, Ainhoa and Xabier's son," the new arrival clarifies, speaking through the bars. He hasn't stopped smiling.

"What's that?"

Markel turns to Katharina now: "Actually, we're second cousins. Our maternal grandfathers were brothers. Virginia was just saying we shouldn't bother you if I wasn't sure we had the right house. But I knew this was it. I've seen lots of pictures. Can't mistake it."

Jon stares at the newcomers. He doesn't move.

"Jontxu," Katharina says. "Open the gate."

He does so reluctantly. His cousin extends his hand.

"What a yard. It looks like a forest. And you have your own cave."

Introductions are made—Virginia, Katharina— and Markel explains that they've just arrived in town. They didn't know the address of the house, but they gave the cab driver Jon's mother's name and said the house was near the Tito Bustillo caves and that was more than enough. The house, in fact, is adjacent to the prehistoric site.

"We've been traveling and, well, let's just say that we wound up here. Your parents aren't home?"

Jon says no.

"Why don't we go up?" Katharina suggests. "It's too cold to talk out here."

"A very good idea," Markel says.

The cousin grabs his own suitcase and Jon has to

deal with Virginia's. It's heavy, and he struggles to lug it up the cobblestone drive. The girl hasn't said a word. She stays one step behind Markel. She glances around constantly, but betrays no hint of emotion.

"Careful," Katharine tells her, pointing at her high heels. "This hill is treacherous."

The girl peers over the top of her sunglasses and nods.

Katharina makes coffee and serves it in the sitting room. Markel explains that he and Virginia have been traveling for three months. They've been in Panama City, Miami, London, and Nice, as well as other, intermediary places, touring and visiting friends. Now they're on their way to Madrid and have stopped to say hello to the family.

"Where do you guys live?" Katharina asks Virginia.

"Santiago de Chile." It's Markel who responds.

"Jontxu, you've never mentioned your cousin."

"Actually, we've never seen each other before," he replies.

Katharina is disconcerted. Markel, seated next to Jon, puts his arm around him, making him spill coffee on the rug.

"But that doesn't matter, does it? We're family. And we've certainly heard a lot about each other, am I right?"

"I don't know about a lot . . ." Jon says.

Sensing his discomfort, Katharina intervenes.

"You don't have a Chilean accent."

"A simple explanation . . ."

"I'll get more coffee," Jon says. In the kitchen, he calls his father.

"Who's there now?" His father sounds delighted. "But why didn't he let us know? We would have come back early to see him."

Then Jon hears how his father holds the receiver away from his mouth and explains what's going on to his mother. He catches her happy exclamation, as well.

"Who did you say he's with? A girlfriend?" his father asks.

"A girl. His partner, I guess."

"He's got a knack with the ladies, that kid. You should keep an eye on Katharina. They'll stay for a few days, right?"

"They didn't say anything about that. Looks like they're passing through."

"Nonsense. Invite them to stay. They're family. Who knows when you'll see him again?"

Jon refrains from saying that he doesn't know or care. Family ties mean less to him than to his father. He hears his mother in the background: *of course, of course they should stay . . . there are more than enough rooms.*

"Have you ever met him, aita? Have you seen him before?"

"Of course! When he was a kid, before he moved to Chile."

His father tells him that Markel is an only child,

and an orphan. Markel's father, an industrial engineer, worked at the phosphate site in Algiers. The father spent extended periods away from his family, who lived in Bilbao. Occasionally, his wife would visit and they'd spend a decent stretch of time together. It was during one of those visits when the small plane carrying the couple to the ruins of Timgad experienced a problem—the nature of which was never clarified—and crashed in the desert. Markel's maternal grandfather, who lived in Santiago de Chile, took him in.

"We're not here on vacation, aita. We're working."

"Don't be silly. It's the weekend. And—I'm just saying—it's not like your jobs are all that critical. Put the kid on the phone. We want to say hi."

Jon returns to the sitting room and holds out the phone to his cousin.

"My parents. They want to talk to you."

The others wait quietly while Markel chats on the phone, smiling all the while.

"No, no we can't . . . seriously . . . they're expecting us in Madrid . . . they'll be mad if we don't go . . . Well, yes, that's true . . . I'll ask Virginia . . . and Jon . . . Katharina, of course . . . Thanks so much . . . You're very kind."

He hands the phone back to Jon, who puts it to his ear. His father has already hung up.

"They invited us to stay for the weekend," Markel says. "But we don't want to be a bother. If you have other plans, we'll go right now."

"We don't have any plans," says Katharina. The cousin has piqued her interest, although she finds him less intriguing than Virginia, whose few words have been monosyllabic. The girl seems to take pains to keep her face expressionless; in any event, she exhibits the wariness of someone facing a task that promises to be boring, unpleasant even. She hasn't taken off her fur coat, just allowed it to slip off her shoulders, her arms still in the sleeves. She's wearing a tight wool turtleneck sweater, black, and black and white houndstooth trousers. Her chest is flat, like a boy's, though there is nothing boyish about the way she moves. Her thighs are as thin as her calves, which makes her legs look even longer. Every time she crosses them, she kicks the coffee table. Markel is wearing the same kind sweater. While they talk, neither one can stifle their yawns; he tries to conceal his, she doesn't. Markel apologizes. They were traveling all night.

"You should stay, of course," Jon says. "My parents invited you and it's their house."

"Jon," Katharina says. "Don't be rude. We're inviting you, too. We're happy to have company."

Suddenly enthused, she looks out the window, claps her hands, and stands on tiptoe, stretching her limbs. The sun is out. She suggests a walk, lunch in town.

"The bedroom downstairs is free," she says. "You can make yourselves at home there."

They haul the luggage downstairs. Still wary, Jon

gives the visitors a tour: bedroom, bathroom for their exclusive use, his father's old office, and the living area, the largest room in the house. Markel admires the fireplace—its marble slabs a gift from a friend of the family, a lay missionary in Burundi— the wood-paneled walls, glass chandeliers, the bookshelves that house the complete works of Zane Grey. But he looks perplexed. He points to the deep alcove set in the back wall, which houses an armchair and reading lamp.

"It wasn't like that before," he says. "There used to be a bar cabinet."

"Could have been," Jon says. "A long time ago. I don't remember."

"And the couches are new. And the blinds. The curtains are gone," Markel says with something that could be interpreted as disappointment. "The furniture has been moved around."

"How do you know that?" Jon asks.

"From the pictures. This house is famous in the family, didn't you know?"

No, Jon acknowledges.

"Make yourselves comfortable," Katharina says. "We'll wait for you upstairs. They won't hold a candle to those in London or Nice, but there are a couple of restaurants in town that aren't bad."

They take them to a place on a back street, avoiding the more touristy restaurants around the harbor. Markel guides the conversation, jumps from anecdote to anecdote, mentions a lot of names, people he knows in the movie business, theater, politics. He takes an interest in Jon's parents and the rest of the family, uncles and aunts, cousins, although there is little Jon can tell him. They speak in Spanish, switching easily to English when Katharina doesn't understand something. They're the type of people who always order a drink on the plane, she thinks, and enjoy it as serenely as they would a cocktail in a hotel bar, even when they're in coach, cushioned always by an aura of superiority.

"You don't drink?" Markel asks her, topping up the wine glasses.

"Not in the mood today," Katharina says, her eyes damp from laughing at one of Markel's stories.

Virginia is still reserved. At least she's removed her fur coat. She's barely spoken, except when it came time to order an aperitif and she ordered Markel to drink wine instead of beer, *it's classier*, and he obeyed. Her accent in Spanish is a mix of Chilean and British English.

"Where are you from, Virginia?" Katharina asks.

Markel answers for her.

"Hull, in Yorkshire. Have you been there? Neither have I, but we're not missing anything, right, Virginia?" Wordlessly, she shakes her head.

Some of what Markel says makes Virginia roll her eyes; with regard to her hosts, they don't seem to have sparked the least bit of curiosity. She ignores them as she eats, filling both cheeks and wiping her mouth on a napkin between bites. Katharina can't stop watching her out the corner of her eye. She's fascinated by the way Virginia's nostrils flare. It reminds Katharina of a thirsty mare sniffing at water. Markel stuffs himself, too; as he talks, he eats and refills his glass and everyone else's. When they get to dessert, the visitors trigger a round of yawns.

"Sorry," Markel says. "Quite the impression we're making."

Katharina suggests returning to the house so they can rest.

As they cross the bridge, they see people down on the Prado de San Juan. They're pitching tents. The prado is a wide, dried-up swath of meadow that extends some two hundred meters down the center of the estuary, before the bridge. Originally marshland, it was fixed up as a recreational site and camping area. A small wooden bridge connects it to the left bank of the estuary, a short distance from Jon's parents' house. The campers appear to be installing some kind of technological equipment.

"I'm going to take a look," Jon says.

Markel offers to join him. The women follow without a word. The campers are rolling out telescopes, cameras and video recording devices, portable weather stations, infrared visors, and Geiger counters. They stop at one of the best-outfitted tents. It belongs to a man and a woman, both elderly, who stoop uncomfortably to pull their devices from airtight storage chests. They wear matching black baseball caps and anoraks with the word VIGILANTES embroidered in yellow.

"What's all this for?" Markel asks.

The old man straightens, wiping his palms on his pant legs.

"Detecting the energetic vortex."

"And, if they come back, to record all the data," the woman adds.

"If who comes back?"

"You don't know?"

Markel replies that he's only just arrived. The ufologists explain what has occurred and show him the pictures from the newspaper on their phone. Markel studies the images with a furrowed brow and then smiles and looks around, as if someone was playing a joke on him.

"Seriously?"

The couple takes no offense.

"A case of mass sightings, the likes of which are rare," the man says.

"Did you guys know about this?" Markel asks.

They witnessed the whole thing, Jon replies, and points to the house, clearly visible from where they stand.

"Witnesses!" says the woman.

"We'd like to ask you some questions." The man pats his pockets. "Where did we put the tape recorder?"

"Did they make any sound when they moved?

A kind of whisper?" the woman asks. "Did any of them shoot sparks?"

"I'm sorry," Jon says. "We have to get going."

"Well, then maybe another time," says the man. "We'll be here for as long as it takes."

"We want to interview the locals. The social environment in which the phenomenon takes place is critical," she adds.

As they return home, Markel has difficulty keeping a smile on his face for the first time since he arrived. He shakes his head, mutters under his breath. They pass more people laden with camping equipment.

"I can't believe how gullible they are," he says, gesturing toward the meadow's occupants. "Don't they have anything better to do? They're adults, for God's sake!"

Back at home, Jon and Katharina leave the visitors downstairs and, wishing them a pleasant rest, go upstairs. Markel comes up a moment later and asks Jon for sheets, blankets, and a pillow. Virginia will sleep on the couch in the living room.

"Is there a problem?"

"No," Markel replies calmly. "It's just that we don't sleep together. We're not a couple."

Jon is clearly confused; Markel clarifies that Virginia is his assistant.

"My grandfather calls her my babysitter, and he's not wrong. I don't know what I'd do without her. I'm useless when it comes to practical matters. On my own, it would just be a matter of days before I wound up broke, or dead."

He explains that Virginia is one of his grandfather's secretaries, and she was offered a raise in exchange for taking care of him on this trip.

"How many secretaries does your grandfather have?"

"Three. But he's had up to five. They fight among themselves. One of them accused another of sabotaging her car brakes. Virginia is better off with me," Markel says, smiling and brushing aside the lock of hair on his forehead.

Katharina listens carefully. She hasn't missed a single detail. Jon hands his cousin the sheets and blankets and accompanies him downstairs to get his laptop and books from his workspace at the living room table.

"Sorry for the bother," Markel says.

"It's not a problem. We have plenty of room."

Jon goes back upstairs. He finds Katharina hiding at the top of the staircase, pressed against the wall at the end of hallway.

"What are you doing?"

She puts a finger to her lips.

They hear the door to the downstairs bathroom open and the click of Virginia's high heels on the living room floor, and how she goes in and shuts the door.

They read for a while in the upstairs sitting room. The house is silent. Katharina gets up more than once and goes to the kitchen, to her room, pauses at the top of the stairs, returns to the sitting room, looks out at the Prado de San Juan, where the number of tents has continued to multiply. Jon watches her, waits for her to say something, but she's focused on her own thoughts. Katharina can't sit still. She gets up and leaves the room again. He puts down his book. He finds Katharina standing before the distressed glass of the old mirror in the hallway, attempting to make her nostrils flare.

"How does she do it? She must have more nose muscles than we do. Where are you going?"

"Something always needs doing in this house."

Jon promised his parents that he would look after the home maintenance and take care of a few repairs in exchange for his stay. He saves the chores for the weekend, but the truth is that up till then his efforts have been largely superficial. He grabs a straw broom and goes outside to sweep the exterior stairs. The house's two floors each have their own terrace. The windows of the downstairs office, bedroom, and living room give onto the lower terrace, which is the largest of the two and actually the roof of the garage. He sweeps it as well. Through the crack in the bedroom curtains, he sees his cousin, sleeping fully clothed in one of the twin beds, one arm thrown across his face. On the other bed, his open suitcase. The living room blinds are closed completely.

Katharina is cleaning in the kitchen.

"Look at you, all house-proud now."

"What's house-proud?"

"Never mind."

"Did you see anything?"

No, he tells her.

Markel and Virginia sleep away the whole afternoon and evening. They come up when Jon and Katharina are setting the table for dinner.

They eat the beef stew from Lorena in the kitchen: Jon has transferred his workspace to the dining room table.

Markel leans on the table with crossed arms and with his usual smile says: "Where did you find a girl like this, Jon?" He looks at Katharina as he speaks. She's changed her clothes and put on a little makeup. Virginia drops her cutlery and takes a sip of wine.

"Is something wrong?" Markel asks her.

She makes a little pout of annoyance and shakes her head.

"Am I misbehaving? Are you going to tell my grandfather?" he says blithely, as if he knows she wouldn't dare. "So," he insists. "How did you two meet? Tell me the story, Katharina."

She inhales and smiles as she lowers her eyes and tucks a lock of hair behind her ear. She explains that they met two years ago, in San Francisco, after they'd both quit their jobs. They fell in love and Jon suggested they move back to Spain. Jon is a mining engineer; upon their return, and to his regret, he resorted to his technical training and took a job at a roller shutter installation and maintenance company. Meanwhile, she translated and copyedited texts; jobs that were always sporadic and poorly paid.

She pauses and looks at Jon, strokes his hand.

"We had a little crisis a few months ago. Jon didn't like repairing shutters. He was as frustrated as he'd been before going to the States."

"That's not what I said."

"Something to that effect. In any case, he left that job, too. And I came to the rescue. I put him in touch with an editorial services company that sometimes sends work my way. They needed people to write the entries for a thematic encyclopedia. They had a hard time finding people with technical knowledge who could write. And so Jon suggested we come to Ribadesella temporarily, to figure out our next step."

Markel inquires what those next steps might be. Katharina says that she would like to get into the audiovisual field, in production.

"But I think it'll be complicated here. I have contacts in Munich, but Jon doesn't want to move."

"Why not?" Markel wants to know.

"My father lives there," Katharina says. "He works in the automotive industry. He promised he could get him a job."

"I guess that doesn't interest you," Markel says to Jon.

"It doesn't interest him at all," Katharina rushes to answer. "Even though my father can find him something part-time that will give him time to write, which is basically what you want, right?"

Jon shrugs noncommittally.

"Are you writing anything now?" Markel asks him. "Besides the encyclopedia."

Jon clicks his tongue.

"No," he says. "I have other things on my mind."

Turning to Katharina, he adds: "And this isn't the time to discuss it."

"We're not discussing anything. Markel asked and I answered. Some of us know how to be polite."

There is a brief silence. For the first time since her arrival, Virginia looks at her hosts with curiosity.

"I get it," Markel says.

He tells them that after he emigrated from Bilbao, his grandfather made his fortune in Chile, first in vineyards and then with a chain of gas stations, obtained in part because of his good relationship with Pinochet.

"I've been working for him ever since I finished my law degree, and I've never liked it."

"That's why you've taken a long vacation," Katharina says, her voice harder now. "And then will you keep working for him?"

Markel looks at Virginia, who remains impassive.

"We'll see," he says as he stretches in his chair, rousting himself, and flashes his huge smile.

"What's your plan?" Katharina asks him.

"Plan . . ." says Markel, as if weighing the word. "Yes, I have a lot of plans. For the time being, we'll keep traveling, right Virginia? Madrid, Sevilla, maybe Marrakesh. But we'll enjoy a few days with you guys first. Not long. I know you have things to do."

"When are you expected in Madrid?" Jon asks.

"Don't know. Midweek?"

"That isn't his way of asking when you'll be leaving," Katharina says as she stands and starts clearing the table.

"Of course not," says Jon. "Here, let me help."

"Don't worry. You guys go to the living room and finish the wine."

Jon and Markel comply, while Virginia stays and helps Katharina.

When they're alone, Virginia asks her if she's pregnant.

"Why do you say that?"

Speaking English, Virginia reminds her that she hasn't had a sip of wine the whole day, adding that she doesn't exactly look like a teetotaler. Katharina admits she's not.

"Wow! Another pregnant woman. Boy or girl?"

"We don't know yet. It's still early."

"Have you thought of names?"

"No. Are you pregnant too?"

Virginia snorts and shakes her head. She's put her plate in the sink and is leaning on the counter while Katharina continues clearing the table. So there are no doubts, Virginia drains the contents of her glass. She glances toward the door. The men are talking in the living room. Lowering her voice, she says that they're not actually on vacation. Markel got someone pregnant who he shouldn't have and his grandfather sent him out of the country until the situation calms down. The girl is the granddaughter of one of the grandfather's business associates, she adds.

"Does Markel love her?"

Virginia studies Katharina with a smile of surprise, amused by the display of sentimentalism. She shakes her head and purses her lips, as if mulling it over.

"I think he does."

"Did she have an abortion?"

Virginia shrugs, tossing her hair, so long it almost reaches the burners. The girl's family doesn't like Markel, she says. Moreover, his grandfather sided with the associate.

"Why don't they like Markel?"

Virginia asks if Katharina likes him.

"I just met him."

Suddenly serious, Virginia leans toward Katharina. Better if it stays that way, she says. Then she looks at the plates stacked in the sink and the tablecloth covered in crumbs, takes a deep sigh, and leaves the kitchen.

Later, when the four of them are gathered in the living room, Katharina suggests a plan for the next day: they could walk to the hermitage of the Virgin de Guía or take an out-of-town daytrip somewhere. Markel praises both ideas. But the next morning, Sunday, he and Virginia sleep until lunchtime and it rains in the afternoon. The visitors spend practically the whole day downstairs. There's no sound from below. Jon takes advantage of the peace and quiet to work on his encyclopedia chapters due the following week.

Katharina puts on her raincoat and leaves the house. She sets off toward the San Juan meadow. Despite the bad weather, the number of tents continues to grow. The ufologists rig up awnings to protect their equipment. The house is just across the way, on the other side of one branch of the estuary. Under the shelter of a large tent, a couple of kids sitting in a circle watch engrossed, as noodles cook on a camp stove. Off to the side, a small generator connected to a sound system hums. A string of colored Christmas lights adorns the tarp extended across the front of the tent. Bottles of rum, gin, and vodka poke out from a couple of plastic grocery bags. Katharina smiles at them and asks if they'll lend her a pair of binoculars.

"Sure," says one. "And if you want something stronger, help yourself."

"Just the binoculars for now."

She takes them and moves a few steps away. She brings the house into focus. The living room blinds are all closed, tight as a drum, as they have been all day. A light is on in Markel's room but she doesn't detect any movement. Then she sees him enter the room, back from the bathroom, she expects. He has a towel around his waist and his hair is wet. He rifles around in the suitcase, chooses some clothes and dries his hair with the towel. As he does, he looks in the direction of the campers with an expression of concentration or displeasure.

"Are you done?"

Katharina turns. One of the kids is standing behind her. He has a narrow face, light brows, child-like features. He's wearing a hooded sweatshirt. He's cold, and self-conscious. Inside the tent, the others watch, laughing and jostling each other.

"Not yet."

"Okay, but we need them back."

"Why?" Katharina asks. She looks through the binoculars again. Markel is putting on pants. "To look for Martians?"

She spies a little longer, ignoring the laughter from inside the tent. She doesn't see him, but she knows the childlike boy is still waiting, and she is increasingly embarrassed. She hands him the bin-oculars. He takes them and Katharina walks back toward the house.

"You're welcome, eh?"

On Monday, there is an incident. Lorena arrives in the morning and is annoyed to find visitors. They should have let her know. The fact that Markel is family doesn't assuage her mistrust. She says a dry hello, giving Virginia a once-over. The girl is wearing another of her turtleneck sweaters, tight jeans, and high-heeled boots.

Lorena takes refuge in the kitchen, leaving the door ajar. "Those heels will mark up the wood floors," they hear her say.

It's raining still. During breakfast, Katharina apologizes as if she's to blame for the weather. Always the optimist, Markel says the sky is lightening up; he has to get back to a few emails, then they can go out. Katharina brightens.

"You can keep working," she tells Jon.

They retire to their rooms. Moments later, they hear shouts from the kitchen. Jon comes out from the dining room and runs into Lorena in the hallway, who has come to find him, tears of indignation in her eyes.

"She threw it out! She threw out the rice I was making!"

She explains how she was cleaning the bathroom while lunch cooked on the stove. When she went to check on the rice, she discovered that the English girl had thrown it in the trash.

"My vegetable rice! My specialty! The one your mother likes so much!"

Jon follows her to the kitchen, where Virginia is waiting at the table. The dish once containing the rice is now in the sink, full of soapy water.

"It was her! She did it!" Lorena insists, peeking out from behind Jon's back.

Alerted by the sound of voices, Katharina and Markel appear.

With absolute composure, Virginia states that the

rice was bad, that Lorena used an expired ingredient. According to Virginia, half the items in the pantry were also expired.

Jon and Katharina can't argue with her. They have no idea what's in the pantry. Except for the occasional whim, they wash their hands of the main shopping and kitchen chores, which they leave to Lorena. The woman asks Jon for grocery money and then a clerk delivers them to the house. The pantry is a realm that Jon and Katharina prefer not to enter. They consider it Lorena's private domain; more a room of her own than a place for storing food. Katharina doesn't like that the woman spends so much time in there with the door closed, taking naps and listening to the radio while she knits. She would prefer that Lorena finish her chores as early as possible and go home. Really, she doesn't even need to come every day. But after so many years of working there, Lorena considers Jon's parents' house to be, in part, hers. She is personally offended that Katharina can't quite manage to be comfortable in the house or in Ribadesella. Katharina is convinced the woman thinks she's spoiled and that Jon could have done better. Lorena often mutters her criticisms when Katharina is within earshot, unaware—or maybe not—that the German girl's command of Spanish gets better every day. Katharina chooses to ignore the commentary, out of courtesy and the desire to keep the tensions to a minimum. She only brought it up to Jon once, and he dismissed it completely, saying that if Katharina had any idea what Lorena's home was like, she'd understand why the woman preferred to spend her days with them. She lives in Cuevas de Agua, over a stable, with no company except her alcoholic husband. For Jon, Lorena is just another part of the house; with time, he's eventually stopped noticing her presence.

"Lies!" says Lorena. "The rice was good. And there's no old food in my pantry. I did the shopping last week."

Virginia drums her nails on the table.

"I'm sure it was a mistake," Jon says.

But Virginia assures him that no, the rice was inedible. Markel intervenes to say that Virginia knows a lot about cooking. Lorena brings a hand to her forehead and twists her apron with the other.

"Never, in all the years I have looked after this house, have I been insulted like this. What will your dear mother say when I tell her!"

Jon tries to calm her, but the woman has no intention of letting the insult slide.

"And you know what else? The Englishwoman told me not to clean downstairs, and with a tone I didn't appreciate one bit."

"It's to save you work," Markel interjects again. "We don't want to be a burden. We can take care of our rooms."

Lorena stares at him as if he'd slapped her. She tries to speak but her indignation is so great, her words come out garbled.

"It's true, we're a lot of people in the house now," Katharina says. "It isn't fair for Lorena to look after everyone. She could take a few days off while Markel and Virginia are here."

"And cook for ourselves?" Jon asks.

"Virginia can handle it," Markel says. "She's a good cook, right?"

Virginia nods and turns her palms up, implying the obvious nature of the suggestion. For her part, Lorena is as horrified as if they were planning out the details of an orgy.

"In that case," Jon says, "let's give it a try. Lorena, why don't you take a few days off."

"What's this? I have to leave?"

"Just for a few days."

"But, when? Now?"

Jon spreads his arms and looks around, as if he doesn't see any reason for her to stick around. "I'll drive you home if you want."

Lorena points a finger at him. "You have never, ever offered to drive me home."

She enters the pantry and slams the door behind her. Virginia repeats that the rice was inedible, pretending to stick her finger down her throat and gag. Katharina stifles her laugher with her hand.

"We should let her collect her things in peace," Jon says.

Behind the house there is an old chicken coop that now serves as a toolshed. Once Lorena has left, Katharina moves her chair from the pantry out there.

Virginia helps. Between the two of them, they clean out the pantry. They don't bother checking the expiration dates; they simply toss out anything they don't like. They fill several trash bags. Virginia finds a pair of Lorena's slippers and a bathrobe. She shows them to Katharina, who shrugs, and Virginia chucks them as well. Then the women and Markel go to the grocery store. Jon stays to work. When they return, he is focused and doesn't get up. He hears them laughing and moving around the kitchen. Later, Katharina calls him to eat and Jon finds the table covered with steaming bowls and dishes. Chilean empanadas, sopa de trillo, chicken stew, fried fish. The sink overflows with pots and pans and the stovetop and countertop are splattered with oil and sauces. The windows are open to air out the smoke. Katharina looks at him, red-faced and slightly out of breath.

"Virginia made pretty much all of it. We just helped."

Jon admits after the first bite that everything is excellent. Markel uncorks one of the bottles of wine they bought. The pantry is once again well-stocked.

"Our way of thanking you for your hospitality," he says. "And as long as we're here, Virginia will also take care of cleaning and tidying the house. Not just our rooms."

Jon and Katharina try to protest, but Markel silences them with a regal gesture.

"There's nothing more to discuss. It's part of Virginia's responsibilities when she's with me."

Virginia merely nods. She looks crestfallen.

"And we'll be leaving soon," Markel adds.

"Why?" Katharina wants to know.

"They're waiting for us in Madrid."

"Nonsense. Call whoever is expecting you. Tell them you're staying a few more days."

Unsure how to respond, Markel looks at Jon. Jon looks at Katharina.

"Why not?" she says. "We still haven't taken them anywhere."

***

They are woken the next morning by a honking horn. Jon goes out onto the upper balcony. Waiting on the other side of the driveway gate is a package delivery truck. He puts on shoes and a robe and heads down the cobblestone slope. The driver checks a dispatch note and reads the name of Jon's cousin.

"Does he live here?"

"He's just visiting."

"Don't matter to me. Do you accept the delivery?"

Jon says yes and asks what it is.

"Could you open the gate here? There's a lot of stuff."

The driver unloads two sets of three suitcases; the first, of sturdy polycarbonate; the second, vintage leather pieces, with shiny brass studs and closed with straps. Then, a makeup carrying case, a large handbag, and a suit bag.

"That's everything," the driver puffs.

One by one, Jon stores the pieces of luggage in the cave for safekeeping.

Back inside, he meets Markel in the kitchen. The coffee pot is burbling away on the stove.

"So our luggage made it," he says, satisfied. "Sometimes we skip around so quickly that it doesn't manage to catch up to us."

They use Jon's car to bring the bags up.

***

They fall into a routine. Virginia gets up early. She spends a couple of hours on housework and then goes out for a run along the beachfront promenade or to the gym in town; often, she does both in one day. The stretches she does at the mouth of the cave look like modeling poses. Everyone she passes stops to look at her. Leggings with transparent cut-outs, cropped sets that expose her midriff, shorts and pink tights. And sunglasses, always, and headphones with the music blasting. In the morning and for part of the afternoon, Jon shuts the door to the dining room and writes drafts of chapters for the encyclopedia. Markel often sleeps past noon. He likes to walk into town, frequent the establishments around the harbor, mingle with the locals, whom he treats to wine and cider so they'll tell him about Ribadesella's history, the salting industry and the sailboats that used to be towed into the harbor by oxen. Katharina joins him. She finally has someone with whom she can waste time in bars. She orders tea for herself but takes sips of Markel's wine. Sometimes they're the bar's only customers. Sometimes the owners get lost back in the storeroom. Sometimes nobody walks by outside for minutes on end. Just the shrieking of gulls. Crates of cider and beer stacked to the ceiling, as if prepared for a siege. It smells like bleach and sawdust, which is sprinkled on the floor. She pushes him to talk about himself. Markel's stories are vague. It's rarely clear when and where the events took place, or if it is clear, it's not clear what he was doing there, in those places populated by people with first names only, names that sometimes come up again but don't seem to correspond to the same people.

They stroll around the harbor. They admire the piles of lobster traps as if they were works of art in a museum. A crab emerges from underneath. They help it return to the water. When the crab gets off course, they step in, make barriers with their feet, heels together, toes turned out, just like Charlie Chaplin. Markel stops a Land Rover on its way to the fish market. The driver complies. He doesn't know what the problem is. When he realizes, he shakes his head and steps on the gas, but by then the crab is safe. It reaches the edge of the docks and drops into the water. The town is too small for them. Passing under sheets hung out to dry, they amble through its back streets, like someone who has drunk to the bottom of a barrel and takes his time with the last bowlful of wine. They press their faces to the grille of the gate at the chapel of Santa Ana. Christ is on the cross, but his arms hang by his sides. The nail through his feet holds him up. It smells like moss and hydrangeas. They buy groceries. Markel pays one day; Katharina pays the next. When it isn't Markel's turn, he insists they go and buy flowers.

When Jon wraps up work in the evening, they go out as a foursome. They drink at the cider house above the Tereñes cliffs. They take off their shoes, roll up their pant legs, and saunter along the beach at Barro at low tide, like sleepwalkers. On the rocks, they peer down into cavities that smell of mud, startling the water fleas. The rocks are irregular and sharp. Their fingers are numb from the cold. They look and discover that they're bleeding, they hadn't even noticed. Sucking the wounds, they ask where they can get something to drink around there.

Virginia's stand-offishness of the first days has tempered. The distance she demonstrates when they are all together is justified by her status as an employee. Everything inspires questions and comments from Markel: the dinosaur ichnites, invisible unless somebody points them out, venison tenderloin seared on the grill . . .

The visitors spend a lot of time downstairs; he in his room and she in the living area, where the blinds are always drawn. They're just resting, Jon and Katharina think; they can't imagine what else they'd be doing.

It takes them several days to realize that Markel and Virginia never leave the house at the same time, unless Jon and Katharina go out as well. They brush it off. At night, they watch movies. They prefer classics, or if not classics, at least ones that are old. They make popcorn and sip whiskey. They watch in the sitting room, lolling about on the sofa, feet on the coffee table. If one starts snoring, the others look at them and smile.

Virginia doesn't participate much in their conversations, but her comments make up for her hours of silence. She doesn't address anybody in particular.

"I like sci-fi movies where there's carpeting in the houses. Even in the spaceships. Like it's the height of modernity."

Her apostilles underscore the complacent, well-intentioned, and predictable nature of Markel's chitchat.

One night, Virginia drinks whiskey straight. She has trouble holding her head up. Markel looks at her condescendingly and asks her if she is comfortable with them. Virginia rests her neck on the back of the chair. Staring at the ceiling, she says she's always had trouble with intimacy. The first time she lived away from her parents, at a boyfriend's house, during the first three months, she went to a pub across the street every time she had to shit.

She stands up, wobbling a bit. She adjusts her bra strap. She looks at each one of them, one by one.

They regard her, fascinated. She begs their pardon and goes downstairs.

Jon is working on an encyclopedia chapter on glaciology. He drafts an outline on a sheet of paper. His pen runs out of ink. He rifles through his papers but finds nothing to write with. There must be something in his father's office.

He descends downstairs as quietly as he can. The door to the living room is closed. Markel comes out of his room to meet him.

"Do you need something?"

"A pen." Jon points to the office.

They go in together. It smells like old paper, wood wax, and typewriter tape. Jon sits behind the desk and opens and closes drawers. He has to pull hard. Some stick, swollen from the damp. The dust makes them sneeze.

A set of curved shelves is stuffed with technical manuals and files. On the desktop, serving as paperweights on top of a few yellowing electricity and water bills, are polished samples of calcium carbonite. They're from the quarry that Jon's father managed until the day he retired, in the Picos de Europa. It was his maternal grandfather who started the extracting, Markel's grandfather's brother. A photograph of Jon's grandfather at the quarry hangs on the wall: a man with a prominent brow, Basque beret, leaning on an iron mallet and surrounded by white stones. The sun beats down. The beret and the heavy forehead shade his eyes. He looks like a prisoner sentenced to do forced labor. Markel takes a seat in the chair on the other side of the desk. Another cloud of dust rises. He waves a hand in front of his nose. On the reverse side of a bill, Jon tests the pens.

"Our grandfathers built this house together," Markel remarks.

"I thought it was just mine," says Jon.

"No, it was the two of them. They bought the land and started building. They designed it so there'd be a floor for each of them. Two kitchens, two separate entrances . . . they were going to mine the quarry together, too. But my grandfather left for Chile before the house was finished. He sold his half of the business and this property to your grandfather."

"I didn't know that. Why did he leave?"

Markel says that his grandfather had qualms about living there.

"He doesn't like to talk about it. Maybe they fought. In any case, things went a lot better for him in Chile than they would've if he'd stayed here crushing rocks."

"My grandfather didn't crush many rocks. He died pretty soon after that picture was taken. It was my father, really, who got the business going."

Jon has already found a pen, but he continues opening up drawers, poking around. He comes across an old slide rule missing a component and a case that holds technical drawing compasses from which half the pieces have disappeared. These were his father's prized possessions, mementos from his student days. Jon played with them when he was a kid, despite being forbidden from being in the office when nobody was there. He ruined them. He doesn't remember his father telling him off. Maybe fatigue and worry over running the business he'd inherited from his father-in-law sapped him of the energy to get angry, which makes the loss even more damnable and produces a decades-late shame.

He leaves a couple of rifle bullets on the table, beside a dark gray piece of metal speckled with greenish flecks. It's long and pointed at the end. It bears the marks of having been chiseled. They found it when they built the drive to reach the house. They've always believed it was the point of a primitive spear, he tells Markel.

Markel asks if he can see it. He runs the pad of his thumb over the jagged edge.

"Shouldn't this be kept somewhere safe?" he asks, handing it back.

"It is," Jon says, and returns it to the drawer.

He explains that the bullets were his father's. He was licensed as a security guard. When they transported the Goma-2 and the ANFO for blasting at the quarry, he escorted the delivery himself. Jon remembers seeing his father arrive home after dark, when Jon was already on his way to bed. His father smelled of motor grease and sweat. His mother was anxious on blast days. His father would call her when it was all done, to reassure her. Those days, his father came home with the rifle or a Smith & Wesson revolver at his waist.

"Do you still have the guns?"

"No. He gave the rifle to a friend who hunts. He turned the revolver over to the Guardia Civil for deactivation. They cut the barrel for him. I suppose it must be around in a closet somewhere."

"You don't take much interest in the family."

"Why do you say that?"

"There's a lot you don't know."

"I take an interest."

"Tell me more."

"About what."

"The family. Your father."

Jon leans back in his chair. Through the window, at Markel's back, he sees the estuary. The tide is in and the sun is shining, gleaming off the branch of the estuary that runs in front of the house; further out, the meadow of San Juan with the ufologist campsites, and on the other side, the dazzling estuary again. He watches one of the ufologists emerge from between the tents, walk to the riverbank, and piss into the water. The swath of reeds bordering the meadow is scattered with litter. Town authorities have provided the campers with chemical toilets and dumpsters, but apparently the estuary is more convenient.

Jon says he's never heard his father intentionally listening to music, nor heard him say that he likes a particular singer or band or composer. He doesn't put on the radio in the car. He's never even heard him speak of music, as if, for him, it was something that didn't exist.

"So silly. Why am I remembering this now?"

It doesn't seem like a bad memory to Markel. Candid, more like. As if Jon's father was a noble savage in a world with no other music than birdsong and where basic needs—shelter, food, the care of his people—left no time for frivolities. Markel has few memories of his own father; he spent little time at home and died when Markel was a child.

"'Don't look at yourself so much in the mirror!' he said to me once. We were at our house, in the living room. He was telling me something, I don't remember what, and instead of looking at him, I was watching myself in the mirror. He startled me. He was so angry all of the sudden. Ashamed."

***

Jon walks past his parents' bedroom and sees that the door is open. Markel is inside, observing the framed photos displayed on the dresser, photos of Jon as a boy, of his parents and grandparents.

"What are you doing?"

"Sorry. I saw the pictures and was curious."

"We usually keep this room closed."

"Virginia must have been dusting in here and left it open, I guess."

On the night tables there are half-read books, tissues, boxes of medication, phone chargers, as if Jon's parents had slept there the night before. Everything waits for their return. Each time they return to Ribadesella, they resume their lives straightaway.

After dinner that night, while they are still sitting around the table, Jon tells Markel that he can show him some old pictures. They're in the sideboard in the downstairs living room. Virginia offers to get them. She comes back with two leatherbound albums and a shoebox full of disorganized photos. They clear off the table and study the pictures, passing them along. When he knows, Jon explains who the people are and when the photo was taken: Jon's mother, very young, with a floral dress and a kitten in each hand; in the background, the house, newly-built, the hillside stripped as yet, bare of the trees and foliage that populate it now. Jon's maternal grandmother, standing on a rock at the edge of the sea, maybe in Ribadesella. She is wearing a long gray dress with short-sleeves and a straw hat. She holds out a pole with a hook at one end, from which hangs a fresh-caught octopus. Jon's mother again, with shorter hair, in the cave beside a trailer carrying his father's fishing boat. She's wearing an apron and holds a can of paint and a brush. The photographs pile up in the middle of the table like discarded playing cards.

"Is this you?" Katharina then asks Jon, who nods. "And who's this with you?"

Jon must be about ten in the picture. He is very brown. Messy, matted hair. Bathing suit and T-shirt. Barefoot. His feet are dirty to the ankles, his knees scraped. He stands against a white wall. The ground underfoot is paved with cement. Beside him, another boy, blond, also in a bathing suit, his shirt unbuttoned. Also against the wall. Also dirty and scraped up.

"I don't know."

"That's me," Markel says.

They all look at the photo.

There's a dog in the foreground at one edge of the frame. Only the back half of it is visible, out of focus. Definitely a German Shepherd. It walked in front of the camera just as the photo was taken. The boys are looking at it with identical expressions: mouth opened in an "O" of surprise and smiling eyes. The dog has turned them into twins.

"I thought you two had never seen each other before," says Katharina.

"That's what I thought," Jon replies.

"Me too," Markel agrees.

"Where is this?" Katharina asks, peering closely at the picture.

"I don't know," they say simultaneously.

They check the shoebox and the albums, but child-Markel doesn't reappear.

Images begin to mount in Jon's memory. He

remembers jumping into the water from the rocks that hug Guadamía beach, where the river of the same name flows into the sea. Someone jumps in after him. The tide is high. For a span of several hours, the river will be converted into a stretch of sea. They swim upstream. Branches of chestnut trees extend out over the water. Small sand beaches no more than a meter-squared and, on one of them, a calf that waits for the tide to go down. A fringe of reed grasses marks the boundary of the brackish water. Banks of limestone scree. Brambles draped like vines. They exit the river to return to the beach on foot, following a cart track. The path bifurcates and they get lost. The ground is muck, a mix of mud and manure. They sink in up to their ankles. They move forward, hanging on to low branches. They reach train tracks and keep to them. Around a bend, they come across a dead badger, head smashed by a train. Jon remembers the smell. They'd sensed it even before they'd reached the curve. It's very hot. The badger is swollen; its testicles like plums. The face of Jon's companion is blurred. A friend? It doesn't look like his cousin. And yet, the photograph has evoked that specific day in detail. The mosquitos on the path, the bluebottles around the cadaver. Could it be that Markel, in the same way that he has appropriated the downstairs, is now taking possession of Jon's memories, replacing images of other people? He strains to remember. The face observing the badger's remains next to his is a hazy mask of superimposed features: two mouths, two noses, three eyes . . . The next time he recalls that day, will it be his cousin's face he sees clearly?

One morning Markel gets up much earlier than usual. He walks into town and comes back by taxi, bearing a 55" screen TV. He can barely maneuver the box up the drive. He explains that it's for Virginia.

"She gets a little bored in the living room."

Jon reminds him that there's a TV in the sitting room upstairs.

"She likes her privacy. It's fine. You guys can keep it later."

Sun's out. Wrap it up.

Jon keeps typing. He knows Katharina is on the other side of the dining room door. He heard the creak of the wood floor.

We're going to leave without you!!!

He'll stop work earlier than usual today. He'd already decided before Katharina started sending messages, but still, he makes her insist; he doesn't want her thinking he's easy to beat.

Where are you going to go without me?

The four of them get in the car, Jon at the wheel. They're going to the beach at Guadamía. The road is narrow. Embankments on either side. They park in a ditch, at such an incline that it feels like the car is about to roll over. They tumble out of the car. The grass is so high that the car doors sweep it down as they open. Closing again, the doors chomp at the grass, as if the car were grazing.

Jon observes Markel. He hasn't said anything to him about the memories the photo sparked. He waits for him to say something, but the visitors simply admire the beach, take pictures. His cousin shows no signs of recognizing the location.

But Jon reels from images and smells, now more intense but no more defined. He's back on the train tracks, looking at the decapitated badger. He feels the mud and cow shit between his toes as it dries, drawing the flies. But he isn't looking at the dead animal. He looks at the boy looking at the dead animal. And that boy is him. He sees himself through the eyes of the person who accompanied him that day.

He chides himself for succumbing to absurdity.

What if Markel and his parents had come for a visit? After all, Jon's parents claim to have met him. Does Jon remember every single one of the cousins who passed through their home when he was a boy? Both his mother and father come from big families. But when they moved to Asturias, contact became less frequent. Jon saw his relatives sporadically, and their visits were always short. To him, they weren't family. They were just guests who came to see his parents, swim at the beach, and eat hake fish in cider. Sometimes they piqued his curiosity; other times, the majority of them, they bored or annoyed him. While the adults ate and drank, he had to act as a guide to those kids and teenagers invading his domain, making a mess of his toys and books, teasing him about his small-town hobbies and few friends. What if Markel had been there, too, and then forgotten, like so many others? What if Markel himself had erased the visit? That would explain everything.

They lie down in the grass. They watch the tide cover the beach. Katharina removes her tights and hikes up her skirt to tan her legs. Virginia flares her nostrils.

"Can you imagine if you guys had come in the summer?" Katharina asks. Parodying exasperation, she clenches her fists, pulls her hair, and slaps Jon on the arm: "Why haven't you ever brought me here? We have to have guests for you to take me out of the house."

She turns to Virginia and Markel. "Don't ever leave."

***

Katharina goes down to the basement for a non-alcoholic beer. They store whatever food doesn't fit in the pantry down there. The basement can be accessed through two doors; one is in the garage, and the other—smaller, she has to duck her head to get through—is inside the house, tucked under the staircase connecting the two floors. Across from the small door is the hallway with Markel's room and the bathroom he and Virginia use. Katharina goes around the house to enter through the garage. While she's down there, she hears the blinds in Markel's room rolling up. She hears his protests. Then she hears Virginia. She puts down the beer. There is fishing equipment on one of the shelves. Inside a glass jar, a few lures with rusty tips. She takes them out, careful not to make noise. The second door is at the back of the basement, at the top of a couple of steep stairs. She climbs up. She sets the mouth of the jar against the door and puts her ear to its bottom. Suddenly, the voices sound clear and close. It's morning; Markel still isn't out of bed; she—Virginia—has gone in to tidy up; she hasn't been able to for days because he's always sleeping; she wants to finish up so she can go to the gym.

"It's fine. I'm getting up."

"   . . .   "

"Virginia? Look."

"   . . .   "

"Check it out . . ."

"   . . .   "

"It's your fault, you know. Me waking up like this."

"Cover yourself."

"Didn't you want me to get up? Put the broom down. Look at me, please. Don't you want it?"

"No."

"Do you ever want it?"

"Son of a bitch."

"Come on . . ."

"I said no."

"You have a good time with me."

" . . . "

"Right?"

"Don't touch me. Get away."

"You touch me, then."

"No."

"Please."

"Don't beg."

"But look at me, I'm . . ."

"I don't want to see it."

"Please."

"Shut up."

"I'll give you fifty euros."

" . . . "

"A hundred. Here."

" . . . "

"Come on. A hundred . . . thirty. I don't have any more on me."

" . . . "

"It'll be quick."

"No."

"All right, you don't have to do anything. Take off your sweater. A hundred and thirty to show me your tits. I love your little-girl titties."

Katharina hears the sound of footsteps quickly approaching. Her heart begins to race. Virginia walks past the door. She climbs the stairs. Katharina doesn't move. She keeps listening. She presses her ear against the glass so hard it hurts, but there's nothing more to hear. She steps carefully down the small set of stairs. One step, pause, one step, pause.

Jon rereads what he has written. His computer, dictionaries, and research take up half the dining room table. Virginia enters the room, dressed in black leggings and a T-shirt. Several strands of hair have escaped her bun. She doesn't speak, doesn't even look at him. She starts to dust, using a feather duster. Jon wonders where she got it. They've never had a feather duster in the house. Did it come with her luggage? Virginia is an apathetic worker. She doesn't tidy—she moves things around. She bends over in front of Jon to dust a chair's sculpted legs. She arranges a lock of hair, which falls back in front of her eyes. She ignores Jon. She positions herself behind him, stretches out her arm, and runs the duster over the books and papers on the table. Her movements are languid. She sidesteps the pieces of furniture intuitively, as if she were in her own home. She pauses before the window. Observing her reflection in the glass, she combs her bangs with her fingers. She might be observing Jon in the reflection. She plucks her leggings from between her butt cheeks. With little sweeps of the feather duster here and there, she leaves the dining room.

***

That night, Jon and Katharina fuck for the first time in weeks.

Later, in the wee hours, Katharina shakes Jon's shoulder.

"What is it?"

"I'm bleeding."

"What?"

It takes him a few seconds to realize what she means. Then he asks: "A lot?"

No, she says. She shows him the panties she's just taken off. She already put on another pair, with a liner. Wordlessly, they get dressed. Jon finds the car keys. As they're just about to leave the house, Katharina asks: "Shouldn't we tell them?"

The downstairs is dark and silent. Jon says they can leave a note. The nighttime cold makes them shiver. They shuffle down the drive, taking short little steps, holding hands.

"Does it hurt?"

"I don't feel anything now."

PART II

Dawn is breaking when they emerge from the hospital in Oviedo. The bleeding has stopped. Katharina still isn't experiencing discomfort. The doctor said that half of pregnancies continue normally after symptoms like hers. She recommends rest. They make the trip back in silence, until he asks: "Are you going to call your parents?"

She thinks.

"It would only make them more unsettled. Will you call yours?"

No, he says, for the same reason.

Later, as they drive into town, she asks: "Are you worried?"

He makes an effort to smile and rubs her knee. "Just the usual."

"And about leaving them alone in the house?"

He says he hasn't thought about it.

Instead of leaving the car in the cave like they normally do, Jon drives it up to the garage, so Katharina won't have to walk up the driveway. Cresting the hill, he slams on the brakes. Katharina is thrown forward; she thrusts out her arms to protect herself from hitting the dashboard but her seatbelt holds her back. The appearance of the car has startled the two German Shepherds in the garage. Markel and Virginia are with them, in their pajamas, bundled up in bomber jackets. Jon almost ran them over. Markel and Virginia have given the dogs water in a cut-glass salad bowl that once belonged to Jon's grandmother. On a couple of plates, leftovers from dinner. Virginia is on her knees. The dogs are licking her face. She looks annoyed at Jon and Katharina for interrupting them. Her cheeks gleam, covered in drool.

Jon steps out of the car.

"How's Katharina?" Markel asks.

"Fine. And these dogs?"

"Edmund and Edgar. We'd left them in Nice. They're very good. They won't be any trouble."

The animals sniff Jon's feet and lap his hands.

"Are they barkers?"

"No. I'm telling you, they won't be any trouble."

Katharina is still in the car. She's in the same position, leaning on the dashboard, appalled.

"Does she need help?" Markel asks.

"She doesn't like dogs."

***

Jon doesn't want to leave Katharina alone. He gives Markel the car keys so he can go to one of the big box home improvement stores on the outskirts of Oviedo. He returns with a doghouse large enough for both animals. It's made of pine and has an asphalt shingle roof. And two gates to place at the top and bottom of the stairs between the two floors, safety gates like those used for babies.

Jon helps Markel install them. One of the times he goes to the kitchen for a beer, he runs into Katharina.

"I told him the dogs can stay, but on the condition that they never come inside. The baby gates are just in case. And they always have to be shut."

Katharina is having tea. She's baggy-eyed.

"They're barricading themselves downstairs."

"Should I tell them to leave?"

She takes a sip and looks out the window. Outside, a seedbed overrun with weeds, limestone outcrops. In the grass under a lemon tree, a water-filled clay pot: a birdbath. Jon's father put it out there to brighten the view from the window. Out of habit, Jon freshens the water every morning. Three sparrows perched on the rim suddenly take flight, startled by a thrush that lands in the center of the pot and adopts a defiant stance, spreads its wings, and opens its beak.

"Wait a little while."

Jon and Markel set up the doghouse. They put it at the back of the garage, next to the boiler room. Jon tells him how they kept the doghouse there, too, when he was a boy. A concrete one, built at the same time as the house.

"You guys had a dog."

"Lots of dogs. Never more than one at a time, but

we always had one, and they were always German Shepherds."

Markel listens, spellbound. Jon says that every time a dog died, his father came back from the quarry with another one a few days later. He doesn't know where he got them. They had one that was part-wolf, and epileptic to boot.

"That one was a problem."

Edmund and Edgar mill around them. Markel has bought them food and water dishes and indestructible rubber toys, though the dogs prefer sniffing the tools, taking the handles in their mouths and carrying them off. Every time Jon needs the hammer, he doesn't know where he's left it. The animals' hips are lower than the German Shepherds he's used to, their bodies more sloped. Markel proudly explains that they are West German Shepherds, a working breed, the specimens closest to the original dogs produced by Max von Stephanitz.

"What happened to the doghouse?"

"Oh, they tore it down. When they put down asphalt in the garage, I think. I still remember how it smelled in there. I used to go in and play. I'd get reprimanded because the smell stuck to my clothes, but I didn't care."

One of the shepherds comes to him and he pets its neck. The animal rolls over onto its back, offering its belly for a rub. The other dog comes running to receive the same treatment.

"What happened to the wolf-dog?"

Jon thinks.

"I don't know. They all blend together. It was always the same dog."

In the afternoon, Katharina says she needs to get out of the house. She needs air. Jon reminds her that the doctor recommended rest. Every time she goes to the bathroom, he asks if she's spotting again.

"So what am I supposed to do? Spend my fucking life inside?"

Jon suggests a walk on the beach. Markel offers to join them.

Katharina doesn't look at him. "I don't want the dogs to come," she says.

"Of course not. They'll stay with Virginia."

As they walk down the hill, Jon asks Markel who Edmund and Edgar belong to.

"Edgar's mine. Edmund is Virginia's. But they both love her more. They adore her. And she adores them."

Katharina is pale. Jon asks if she's cold.

"No. Let's go," she says.

They walk along the side of the road. As they're rounding the first bend, a pair of ufologists comes out to greet them. The same ones Jon and Markel spoke to on the Prado de San Juan, the old couple with the VIGILANTES hats.

"Good afternoon," they smile. "We waited for you."

"What for?" Jon asks.

"Don't you remember us? You agreed that we could interview you."

"We didn't agree to anything," Jon says.

"It will just take a minute," the man insists. "Just a couple of specific questions. Serious ones. Our work is scientifically rigorous. We don't allow ourselves to be carried away by assumptions and prejudice."

"Not like some of the others," the woman adds.

"Sorry, but it's not a good time," Jon says.

"Where are you headed?" the woman asks. "We could walk with you and talk on the way."

"Excuse us," Jon says. Taking Katharina's arm, he sets off.

"My apologies if we've annoyed you," the man says. "Would you prefer to talk another time? You can trust us."

Markel intervenes. "Leave these people alone."

The woman responds by raising her voice: "You have had the honor and the grace to witness the celestial brothers. Why don't you want to spread the message?"

"What's your problem?" Markel says. "Can't you see they don't want to talk to you? Just leave them alone."

Markel motions for Jon and Katharina to keep walking. Then he turns, walking backward to make sure the VIGILANTES don't follow.

"They will escort Jesus Christ on His return to Earth!" they hear the woman shout.

Markel catches up to Jon and Katharina after a couple hundred meters.

"We don't have to worry, not with the dogs at the house. They're good guard dogs. They'll scare off any looky-loos."

The couple doesn't answer.

They meet more ufologists along the way, but these ones don't pay them any attention. Some push grocery carts, which local businesses have lent them so they can bring their shopping back to the Prado de San Juan. The first days, the neighbors of Ribadesella had looked at the campers with mistrust and some degree of derision. Now they have accepted them. The ufologists head into town each day, talking with locals and looking for evidence left by the flying objects, or anything that could be interpreted as a consequence of their appearance: sudden migrations of birds or the presence of dead fish on the beach. They've found nothing, for the moment. No new events have occurred in the skies. Each time a jet plane's contrail appears over the town, the ufologists anxiously point their cameras. While they wait for something to happen, they drink in the bars and buy at the shops; for the town, they represent a source of income and excitement in the traditionally gloomy period before the Easter holidays.

Upon their return, Katharina, Jon, and Markel find a piece of paper stuck in the gap between the double doors of the gate. It's a page torn out of a notebook: "'I will spew the lukewarm from my mouth,' said the Lord."

New notes appear the following days: "Don't participate in the cover-up," "The Lords of the Stars, equipped with antimatter annihilation engines, will receive detailed word of you and your recalcitrance."

"Are the dogs tied up?" Katharina asks.

"Why?" says Virginia.

"I'm going out. To the grocery store."

Virginia says the dogs won't do anything. Even so, Katharina insists.

"It's my house. I want them tied up."

Virginia leaves the veal cutlets she's breading and goes to look for the dogs, but not before reminding Katharina that the house is not hers. The two women are alone; Jon and Markel have gone out.

Katharina waits impatiently, watching from the kitchen window. Virginia is gone a while. The sky over the sea is heavy with dark clouds. After the grocery store, Katharina wants to stretch her legs with a stroll through the harbor. Virginia comes back at last.

"You can go out now."

Katharina doesn't say goodbye.

The sky is now completely overcast. Katharina has decided to dispense with the walk. Once her errands are done, she goes straight home. She parks in the cave. She beeps the horn a few times, which she usually does to get somebody to come down and help her with the bags. No answer. She beeps again, with the same result. She walks up, carrying two bags in each hand. She tries to ignore the clinking of the dogs' chains. When she reaches the garage, she turns toward the stairs that lead up to the house without looking at the animals. The house has three entrances: the basement door; a door on the lower balcony, which leads to the downstairs, occupied by the guests; and the door that allows direct entry to the upstairs. This is the one Jon and Katharina use. The handles on the bags are cutting off circulation to her fingers. She has to take several breaks. She stops again when she is about to reach the door, out of breath. At her feet, a snake slithers out of the crate where they store the gas canisters. It crawls off into the high grass. She has come across snakes outside before: remains abandoned by owls, bodies missing pieces or slit down the middle, revealing violet guts. This snake is different. From a distance she can make out the scales, perfectly discernible, steel-like. The scratch of its belly on the cement path produces a raspy sound. It is as thick as a child's arm and a meter-long at least, maybe more. Even when she can no longer see the reptile, Katharina can follow its movements by the rustling of the vegetation, bushes, and saplings of considerable size.

She moves forward cautiously. She enters the house and rushes to the kitchen. She drops the load of bags on the table just as they are about to escape her grip. A kilo of plums rolls onto the floor. A can of tomato sauce follows suit, and when it crashes on the tiles Katharina jumps and stares, waiting for the red stain to spread to her feet. She thinks of the snake. She looks out the window. The bird bath is deserted.

She is startled again, this time by Virginia's voice, asking her what's wrong.

"Where were you?"

Taking a nap, Virginia replies. She steps aside just in time to avoid being bowled over by Katharina, who hurries out of the kitchen.

Katharina does a run-through of the upstairs to make sure there are no open windows, and as she does so, she casts leery glances at the intricate patterns featuring the colors green, brown, or black.

What color was it? Did it have a design? A sort of horn on its nose? Was the head triangle-shaped, or round? Jon is back and every question he asks makes Katharina angrier.

"I don't know. It was a fucking snake. Go outside and kill it."

Markel suggests they bring the dogs. Virginia refuses, Edmund and Edgar can't go out with them, not with a viper about.

"I don't think it's a viper," Jon says. "I'm sure it was a garden snake. They can get really big sometimes."

From the old chicken coop, he takes an ax and a shovel. He offers them to Markel, who chooses the ax. It has started to thunder. From the garage, the dogs bark in response to each rumble. Jon and Markel wade into the vegetation in the area where the snake disappeared. Katharina and Virginia watch from the kitchen window. Virginia opens it and says something about brave men rescuing damsels in distress. Katharina is silent. The men don't answer, either. They advance forward with their eyes trained on the ground, pushing aside the tall grass with the tools. Rain starts to fall. There are no drops to serve as a warning. All at once, it's a driving rain that's unleashed. Jon and Markel run back, soaked by the time they get inside.

It rains through the rest of the afternoon and all night. It's still raining the next day. Night falls as they drink hot chocolate, the four of them, in the sitting room. Virginia made it. She added cinnamon. She's cross. She asks more than once if the dogs can come inside. She promises they will stay downstairs, but Markel has remained firm. He says that they're safe and sound in the doghouse. They swirl the chocolate around in their mugs, sweeping up the cinnamon stuck on the inside. Katharina is seated, legs tucked under her and covered with a blanket. She stares out the window toward the Prado de San Juan, where everything is still. She says that, on nights like this, she likes the house even less. Another clap of thunder. Storm fronts chasing each other's heels. Jon muses out loud about a similar stretch of bad weather, from when he was a boy. He tells them that before his grandfather built the house, the site used to be a rudimentary brickworks where clay was extracted from a vein running down the mountainside. That time it rained so hard that the clay started to shift, producing a landslide. When he went to the bathroom that night, he lifted the lid on the toilet and found mice in the bowl. A dozen or so. Almost all had drowned; a few were still treading water. Fleeing the rain and the clay, they had somehow gotten into the pipes. He flushed the toilet over and over, until they all disappeared.

"Great," Katharina says. "I had to pee and now I can't. No way."

The windows light up, pure white. Instantly, a clap of thunder starts with a crackling sound and builds. The lights go out. Jon cranes his neck. The town is also dark.

"We'll wait," he whispers.

The echo lingers. The darkness is absolute and there is no more lightning.

After a moment, Jon goes to the kitchen, his cell-phone lighting the way. He returns with a lighter. On the fireplace mantel stands a three-armed candelabra. He lights the wicks. They are silent, observing the little flames, the soft wax drips, until the streetlights go back on. The house, nonetheless, remains dark.

"I'll go check," Jon says.

"Do you want some help?" Markel asks.

"With what?"

The circuit breaker is downstairs. He doesn't say so to the guests. He grabs a flashlight they keep in the pantry. He opens the baby gate and walks downstairs as quietly as he can. He opens the second gate. He goes into the study. The breaker is behind the door. All the magnetothermic switches are in the up position. The problem is outside. Before heading back upstairs, he puts his hand on the knob on the door to the downstairs living room. It swings open easily. He waits. He hears the others talking in the sitting room above. He steps into the living room and shuts the door. He turns off the flashlight and uses his phone, to be more discreet.

He has trouble recognizing the room. Even the odor is different: heavy and sour. The furniture has been moved. The couch is being used as a bed, the sheets and blankets are in disarray. The coffee table is taken up by the new TV and has been moved to be seen better from the couch. The rolling shutters, as always, are down. It's the mess he finds shocking. Suitcases are open on the floor; the two sets that arrived after the guests, and their contents are found strewn on all surfaces. Clothes hanging on the backs of chairs, on the armchairs, piled on the table where Jon used to work, single shoes missing their pair, lingerie and coats and jackets heaped together, wrinkled, all of it, and scattered on the floor amid used Kleenex, wet wipes, empty beer cans and wine bottles, chocolate wrappers, bags of potato chips, hairbrushes, fashion magazines, open tubes of makeup . . . It's impossible to move without stepping on something. Among the clothing, there are items with the tags still on. Shoes with pristine soles. He bends to pick one up. A Louboutin. He sees a ficus lying under a radiator, along with its soil, now spilled. It used to be in a large ornamental flowerpot. He finds the pot by the end of the couch. Beside it, a roll of toilet paper. He peers inside. Urine fills it halfway to the top.

He sees a bowl with dog food. Despite being expressly forbidden, Virginia is letting the dogs in the house. She must take advantage when he and Katharina go out.

His attention is drawn to the bag on the couch. Sticking out is a gray cardboard binder. It looks old. He opens it. The pages are yellowed. Some paragraphs are type-written, others by hand, in spiky, sharply slanted lettering. He reads family names. Official stamps. The deed to the house. He hesitates then returns the binder to the bag. He wants to keep searching, but the mess makes it hard to know where. And he's been gone a long time. He leaves the living room. He switches the flashlight back on and heads upstairs. At the very moment he enters the sitting room, the lamps turn on, weak at first, before regaining their usual brightness.

"You bring the light," Markel says.

A short time later, as they eat dinner in the kitchen, Jon raises his finger.

"Listen."

The rain has stopped.

They go out behind the house and breathe as if they've been shut in for weeks. The water trickling down the mountainside produces a whisper-sound, like circulating blood.

"Shall we let the dogs out?" Virginia suggests.

Markel nods. She goes down to the garage. Katharina takes refuge in the house. Markel and Jon fill their lungs with the aroma of saturated earth. They hear the dogs racing up the stairs, getting in each other's way, barking like a whole pack of hounds. The animals bound uphill, muzzles in the air, paws kicking up mud. They roll in the grass. The clouds retract. The moon materializes, shading all in indigo blue. Virginia returns, hugging herself to keep warm. The dogs are getting dirty, she says. With envy, Jon and Markel watch the animals frolic.

"Let them," Markel says. "They need the exercise."

Virginian sniffs and goes inside. A stray rumble of thunder reverberates, the parting shot of a storm in retreat. One of the dogs puts its tail between its legs. The other sniffs the ground, digs, runs about, enjoying itself.

"That one's Edgar," Markel says. "My dog. I'll go with them. You?"

"We'll get soaked."

"Don't you want to stretch your legs? I do."

Jon puts on the shoes he uses to work in the yard. He finds a pair of his father's rain boots for Markel.

"They fit okay?"

"Perfect. Let's go."

Steps have been dug into the dirt in order to access the property from the balconies; they're difficult to find in the dark, in the overgrown grass. Jon and Markel clutch at tree branches, rocks, each other. They slip and fall, with little consequence other than wet pants. They didn't even take their coats, or flashlights either. At their approach, the dogs redouble their frenzy.

Suddenly, Markel stops short and looks around in alarm.

"And the viper?" he whispers.

"There's probably no viper. And it will be tucked up in some hole by now. Snakes don't like the cold."

Jon remembers a trick he used to use to attract garden snakes and slow-worms: fill balloons with hot water and leave them in the grass or under bushes. He says that they could do the same thing now. Markel is enthused by the idea. His voice, once a whisper, returns to normal. As they climb, he asks what they would do next, would they hide and wait for the snake with the ax and shovel?

At the top of the hill, Jon warns Markel to be careful where he steps. A low, dry-stone wall marks the property boundary. Running parallel, a line of eucalyptus. The trees rustle, rocked by the winds that trail the storm. The ground is covered in acorns. Where the concentration is greatest, it's like walking on ball bearings. Markel hugs one of the trees and lets himself slide until he can sit on the stone wall, springy with dry leaves and bark fibers. Jon does the same. The dogs lie at his feet, lapping their paws and running them over their muzzles, like cats. Dotting the hillside, limestone poking out like teeth in a baby's gums. A cloud passes in front of the moon.

The glints of moonlight on the estuary disappear. The lights in town become more visible, less diffuse. The hills hugging the estuary darken. At the house below, the back door opens and Katharina steps out, looking for them. It's unlikely she can see them in the dark, concealed by the trees. Still, they stay quiet, motionless, holding their breath, the two men and the two dogs. If she spots them, she'll tell them to come back, that it's cold out, that it's late. She returns inside and shuts the door.

"What's over there?" Markel asks, pointing behind them, to the other side the wall.

A chestnut grove, Jon tells him. And the sinkhole where the runoff filters down into the mountain's interior, like a drain; and a network of ditches, trenches, possibly, from the Civil War. He used to play there as a child, but it's been years since he climbed over the wall. The ground is uneven, nobody looks after it, it's been annexed by weeds and brush.

They are quiet until Jon says: "I'm thinking about asking Lorena to come back. I don't think it's right for Virginia to keep taking care of the house. And Katharina and I have to work. She can't do much in her condition, anyway."

Markel assures him that he shouldn't worry; Virginia can take care of everything.

Jon pets one of the German Shepherds. Its fur is damp. He wipes his hand on the leg of his pants, also damp. In the end, he dries his hand on his sweater.

"Don't get me wrong. I appreciate Virginia

cooking and cleaning, but I've noticed that, in terms of the cleaning . . ."

"What?"

"Well, it's a demanding house. You have to know it, know how to tackle it. I can't ask Virginia to climb up a ladder to sweep cobwebs from the eaves."

"I hadn't noticed the eaves. Is there something else she should be doing that she's not?"

"Don't get upset. There are a couple of things. The house is getting dirtier and dirtier. Katharina is pregnant. I don't want her living in those conditions."

Markel says he understands.

"We're paying Lorena anyway. She doesn't have to come every day. Just to do the deep cleaning. It's better for everyone."

Markel takes time to respond. When he does, his smile burns bright, even through the night.

"You're right. It's just that we're so good on our own, the four of us."

"Then I can have a word with Virginia. Give her some pointers. Or help her out."

"No." Markel is suddenly serious. "Don't say anything. I'll talk to her."

"Why not?"

"You don't know her. She's demanding, too. If you tell her that Lorena's coming back, she'll be mad. And she'll be mad if you tell her that she doesn't clean like she should. Leave it me. I'm used to negotiating with her."

The moon is back out.

"Let's head down," Jon says. "While there's light." As if they understood him, the dogs get up and lead the way.

Markel, however, remains on the wall.

"Be careful with Virginia," he says. "You guys don't want to see her angry. I have to admit, she scares me. She can be poisonous. Tell Katharina."

***

Katharina is kneeling on the bed. "You did the right thing," she says when Jon tells her what happened: the visit to the living room and the chat with Markel.

He's not so sure. He thinks he should have taken the deed. And maybe he should have talked to Markel about it, as well. Though it's possible he doesn't know. Jon is sure that Virginia, with the excuse of cleaning, searched the house until she found the document.

Katharina asks him to describe the living room again. She looks off in the distance as he speaks, now smiling, now disgusted, now smiling again, in disbelief that such mess and neglect are just a few yards away.

"Let's see what they do now," she says.

Jon nods. He doesn't mention that Virginia lets the German Shepherds inside.

"Did you go in his room?"

No, Jon says. In any case, Markel leaves the blinds up, he opens his windows. Jon has taken a peek from the outside on a couple of occasions, and he knows Katharina has done the same.

"Oh, and I don't want Lorena to come back either," she concludes. "Even if we're overflowing with filth."

In the morning, the Prado de San Juan is a pitiful sight. Some of the tents have collapsed under the weight of the rain. Dejected campers wander around, avoiding puddles, wrapped in blankets. A few pack up their equipment. The insufficient dumpsters are filled to the top. The town hasn't emptied them in days. Seagulls swoop upon the trash, scattering it. The swollen estuary is receding again. It seems on the brink of swamping the grass and sweeping away the remnants of the camp.

Katharina is spending a lot of time in the basement. She enters through the garage, after confirming that no one has seen her. She doesn't make any noise. Doesn't switch on the overhead bulb. She uses her cellphone to light her way, keeping it to a minimum. She's afraid the light will leak through the slats of the door to the downstairs. She climbs up the short set of stairs. If she hears voices, she holds the mouth of a glass to the door and listens through the other end. But most of the time she just stays here and sits. There is no lock, no latch, on the door. Anyone on the other side could open it. This, in the beginning, arouses her. She is always careful to silence her phone.

After several days of surveillance, however, she finds a board left over from some repairwork and uses it to brace the door, positioning one end under the doorknob and jamming the other against the facing wall.

She communicates with Jon via text. He warns her if the visitors go downstairs. When she wants to retreat, she asks him if the coast is clear. This game excites them.

In the dark, perched on the last stair, her buttocks numb, she lets her imagination soar beyond what she dares to do in her conversations with Jon. She considers things she would never say to him, for fear he would think her prissy and outlandish.

She almost never hears anything beyond footsteps, the open and closing of doors, the toilet tank in the bathroom, bed springs. Why do those two barely speak to one another? What have they done all this time they've been traveling? If it's even true, of course, that they've been travelling the world at all.

The house is quiet. Still drowsy from the siesta, Katharina leaves the bedroom. She picks up balls of hair and dust in the hallways and throws them in the trash. The plates from breakfast and lunch are still in the kitchen sink. They had frozen pizzas. Virginia dedicates less and less time to her domestic tasks.

She pops her head into the dining room, but Jon isn't there. His computer is off. She remembers he said he would go into town with Markel to buy a BEWARE OF DOG sign for the gate. They hope it will dissuade the ufologists from leaving more notes. She decides to go back to her room and read.

Passing the stairs, she glances downstairs as usual. She stops. One of the dogs is in the entryway on the lower level. She isn't sure if its Edgar or Edmund. The two safety gates are closed. The dog looks at her, wagging its tail. Katharina gestures for it to go away. Effortlessly, the German Shepherd jumps over the lower gate, runs up the stairs, its nails digging into the wood. Katharina steps back in fear. The dog reaches the second gate, but this time the animal can't clear it. Half its body is on one side of the gate and half on the other, its haunches stuck on the upper crossbar. The dog manages to get its front paws on the floor. The back legs twitch as it yelps in pain.

Katharina rushes to the door outside. She flings it open but stops, paralyzed. Before her, on the stone steps leading to the old chicken coop, the other dog waits. From its mouth hangs the lifeless body of a snake, the same one Katharina saw. The dog's teeth clasp the serpent by the middle of its body. Its tail trails on the ground; the head, a gnawed jumble, does too. Dog drool drips down the carcass and mingles with the reptile's blood.

The fasteners securing the gate buckle under the weight of the first dog. Animal and gate crash down with a clatter as Katharina screams.

Cornered, her only escape is the tiny half-bath in

the entryway. She lunges inside, sliding the latch shut. The dog scratches at the door and barks. Through the privacy glass window, she sees the deformed silhouette of the other animal, growling and snorting while appearing to either rip the snake into pieces or devour it. Katharina cries for help. No one answers. Her phone is in the bedroom, so she can't call Jon. But Virginia should be home. She shouts the woman's name. She pounds on the door, only further riling the dog on the other side. She feels on the verge of a panic attack. Her ears ring and she struggles to breathe. She dampens her face with cold water. Again, she shouts for Virginia. She sits on the toilet and concentrates on slowing her breath. Soon she no longer hears the dogs, but she doesn't dare leave the bathroom.

Half an hour later, she hears Virginia coming up the stairs, asking Edmund what he's doing there.

"Take that fucking dog outside!"

"Katharina?"

"Take him out."

Virginia asks what she's doing locked in the bathroom. It sounds like she's trying not to laugh.

"Take him with you!"

Virginia says she's going, not to get angry.

"Take them both! I wanted them tied up!"

Katharina hears Virginia leave the house with the animals. Still, she doesn't come out. She waits for Virginia to get back. It feels like an eternity.

"What were you doing? I was calling you. Didn't you hear me?"

Virginia tells her that she was in the shower.

"The whole time? Your hair is dry."

She didn't wash it, Virginia says.

***

The tectonic plate in the Caribbean comprises the con-
tinental part of Central America and the bottom of
the Caribbean Sea. Its surface is approximately 3.2
million square kilometers. To the north, it borders the
North American plate; to the east and south, the South
American; and to the west, the Cocos plate. Its borders
are active in terms of volcanic eruptions and seismic
movement.

The dining room chairs are not comfortable.
Chestnut, ornate. Jon cushions them with pillows,
but it's not enough. He hears a door close. He looks
at the clock. Virginia is back from her run. Silence
again. Like Katharina always says, with silence you
sense everything more. She means the dampness in
the house, the tickle of dust in your nose holding you
captive on the brink of a sneeze. He notes the ten-
sion in his back, between the shoulder blades, sharp
and precise, as if someone were pinching him. He
envisions a bony thumb and pointer finger, greenish knuckles and ragged nails, boring into the flesh
on either side of his spine. He stands and goes to
the window. At the gate below, someone dressed in
black, head covered by a hood, is leaving a note. Jon
runs outside.

"Hey! You!"

The stranger is heading in the direction of the Prado de San Juan; they stop, look back. The first thing Jon sees is the jacket: VIGILANTES. The woman is worse for the wear after days of camping. She looks disheveled and haggard. She coughs discreetly to one side. She attempts a smile but is unsuccessful, a result of exhaustion more than fear. Jon strides toward her.

"I know you! I know your tent!" he blurts, and immediately feels ridiculous. He reins in his voice. Releasing his inner engineer, he adds coldly: "Do not leave another note. If you do, I'll call the Guardia Civil."

She isn't intimidated. A northeasterly wind is whipping. She holds down the hood of her anorak over her ears.

"I don't understand how you can turn your back on the Brothers in the Sky. We won't have another opportunity like this."

Jon is about to ask what she means by opportunity, but he contains himself.

"Can't you see that your refusal might hinder their return?" she presses.

"Don't come around here again."

The woman shakes her head. She looks out at the estuary and the campers on the Prado de San Juan. She squints, trying to make something out. Then she turns to Jon and takes a step closer. In an undertone she says: "Truth is, I wanted to talk to you without my husband. I have information that will convince you of the magnitude of what has happened—and will hopefully happen again."

She adds that she has better, more intriguing proof than what her husband can offer. She says that she is in possession of documents and asks if they can meet in private, in town maybe, so she can show him the evidence and translate it for him.

Jon looks back at the house. He stretches his jaw, moving it from side to side.

"We have dogs. If I see you or your husband again, I'll let them out."

He turns around. He rips the woman's note from the gate, crumples it into a ball, and chucks it into the road.

When he goes inside, brooding over what the ufologist said, more unsettled than when he went out after her, he stops short before reaching the dining room.

"Hi."

"Hi."

The anger is suddenly gone, replaced by the sense of astonishment at seeing a nearly-naked woman, an attractive woman, practically a stranger, in his parents' hallway, where he played as a child. As rare a sight as the flying saucers. Virginia is wearing a pink sports bra and a white thong. She's sweating. She holds her running shoes in one hand. Not taking her eyes off Jon, she lets them drop. She stands with her arms by her side. One knee forward, toes pointed on the floor. She pretends to hear something behind her and turns to show him her ass.

Jon looks around. Where are Markel and Katharina?

"Hi," she says again. And after a pause: "Thanks for getting rid of that crazy woman."

"You know her?"

"I've seen her."

"Leaving notes?"

Virginia nods.

"Why didn't you warn us?"

"She didn't seem dangerous. And besides, I figured there was already somebody who could take care of it properly. Much better than I would."

Her voice is deep, almost a purr.

"Do you usually walk around the house like that?"

"When nobody's home."

"You knew I was here."

She smiles and wipes the sweat from her forehead.

"Do you want me to clean something? Dust the dining room?"

He studies her at length. He grants himself that, at least. Logs the details. Then he shakes his head, and steps into the dining room.

"You'll regret it," Virginia says before he can shut the door. "Tonight, in bed, you'll regret it."

"I might," he says. "But I'll feel good when I wake up tomorrow. And what matters is how you feel the next day."

He waits behind the closed door until he hears the girl move away. He peeks out into the hall. All clear. He goes to the kitchen and gets a beer.

He suppresses the urge to think about Virginia and Markel again, to try and remember if he ever met his cousin, to take the fluff from another pair of lives and use it to fashion a fiction, to sublimate people into characters. That's not why they're there. And he has work to do.

The septentrional edge of the plate, in its union with the North American, represents a transformative border. It runs the length of Belize, Guatemala, and Honduras, then enters the Caribbean from the east, passing along southern Cuba and the north of Hispaniola, Puerto Rico, and the Virgin Islands.

Katharina hasn't translated anything in days. She decided she won't be continuing with the job, even though she hasn't told the editing services company yet. It doesn't matter if they refuse to pay her for the chapters she's already finished. She hasn't even said anything to Jon, though she expects he's figured it out. In spite of the visitors and all that's happened, he continues to turn in his weekly quota of encyclopedia entries.

"Will you come to the grocery store with me?" she asks over breakfast.

They are alone in the kitchen. She wants to spend some time with him, she adds, outside the house, doing something normal. Jon thinks it's a good idea. He can start work later that morning, or not work at all. All at once she is happy: it was that easy.

They take the car into town. In the first shop, Katharina says she feels dizzy. Jon offers to bring her back home, but no, she says, she prefers to walk. The air will do her good. She assures him there's no need to worry and reminds him of a few things they need that aren't on the list.

She exits the shop. She checks that Jon can't see her and quickens her pace. When they left the house, Markel and Virginia hadn't been up yet. They left a note where they'll be sure to see it.

She monitors the house through the grille on the front gate, in case the dogs are loose. She doesn't see or hear them. She climbs the driveway to the garage, which smells like dog shit. The German Shepherds aren't inside. Edgar and Edmund have pulled out the pieces of cardboard Virginia used to cover the floor of the doghouse and destroyed them. Paw-trampled excrement everywhere.

She can hear them fucking as soon as she enters the basement. They're in Markel's room. Her heart pounds as she climbs the couple of stairs to the door. She doesn't need the glass to hear them, but she uses it anyway, the one she keeps there for that purpose. The instant she presses it to her ear, it's like she's there with them. Virginia's rhythmic moans, the shudder of the bed frame, the smack of a hand on an ass cheek; there is a short, sharp cry and then the moaning returns.

Katharina is so absorbed that she doesn't hear the other sounds, or doesn't register them, until they are but a few centimeters away, hideously amplified by the jar. Edgar and Edmund are sniffing the bottom of the door, scratching at the wood floor. She almost drops the glass, which would have shattered on the basement floor and given her away. Or perhaps not, because Virginia and Markel don't notice until one of the dogs whines and Virginia, in a choked voice, asks what's wrong. Markel ignores her. The bed keeps creaking. Now the dogs are barking. Not threatening barks. More like signaling. They alternate, Edgar, Edmund, Edgar . . . *Katharina! Katharina!* they would say if they could speak.

"What is it?" Virginia says. "Edmund?"

"I'm so close," Markel says. "Don't move."

New moans. Suffocated. Pained. Mixed with the Shepherds' yowls.

"Let go of me!"

Two shudders, three, and the bed is quiet. Steps in the hall. By now, Katharina recognizes his footfall perfectly. The bathroom door closing. More steps. These ones are coming near. Bare feet on the wood. Virginia scolds the dogs. She asks them what's wrong. Katharina hears them move away. She imagines Virginia dragging them by the collar. But they don't go far. The bathroom door opens. Markel asks what all the fuss is. Katharina has taken the glass off the door, she clutches it in her hands. She hears their conversation without it. Markel says they have to get the dogs out of there. He doesn't want those two to come home and find them in the house. The situation is complicated enough already. He'll do it, he says, he wants to get something to eat upstairs, hopefully they've made coffee. He asks Virginia to wait while he gets dressed. A moment of silence and then Markel takes the dogs, who don't stop whining, slipping on the wood floor.

It's a good time for Katharina to get going.

But before she can take a single step down, she's startled again. The sound is unmistakable. Still she can't be certain because the sound of her own pulse is just as loud. Later, she will be surprised by how she reacts. She uses the light of her phone to illuminate the door handle, confirming that the noise corresponds to what she thought: it's the handle, moving up and down. Virginia, she surmises, has crept up to the door.

The door won't open: the bracing board holds. Katharina stays put, though she has time to climb down, leave the garage, and go inside. Pretend she's none the wiser. She hugs the board to make sure it doesn't shift. Silence, all of a sudden. The handle is still. Several seconds go by. She lets go of the board.

The handle begins to move again, faster. She grips the board. Then another pause.

She can leave, she thinks.

In any case, what if the board were to give, the

door to open, and Virginia to discover her there? What would happen? She could easily invent a simple excuse to explain her presence.

But Katharina is not a fan of excuses, so she prefers to stay, cramped, sweaty-faced, hair plastered to her forehead. This is her partner's house and she can do whatever she wants.

She releases the board and leans back against the wall. The handle continues to move intermittently. A long pause. The handle. A longer pause. The handle, up-down, up-down. Katharina stares at the door in the dark, waiting for a light to blind her, a silhouette of a figure on guard.

Gradually, she becomes calm. Closes her eyes. She doesn't check the time. She doesn't even react when, finally, the handle's movement is replaced with a light rapping of knuckles on the door. Polite. Cowed, even.

She climbs down the steps. Leaves the garage. She circles the house and enters through the door to the upstairs; proud, she makes no effort to quiet her footsteps. She goes to the bathroom to freshen up. There is pleasure in the sensation of cold water on her face, the drips that slide down between her breasts and wet her bra, already soaked in sweat.

"Wake up . . . Jon, wake up!"

"What is it?"

It's the middle of the night. They've all been

asleep for hours. Katharina is standing beside the bed.

"I'm bleeding."

"What? Like before?"

"No. More."

She was awoken by a pang in her lower back. Then she felt the wetness.

Jon manages to turn on the bedside lamp. They contemplate the blood on the sheet.

Her voice is grave. "It doesn't hurt anymore."

PART III

"WOULD YOU GUYS MIND if we stayed a little longer? Just a couple of days."

Jon doesn't answer. He's making breakfast.

Apologetically, Markel continues: "The friends we were going to see in Madrid have had a problem. It wouldn't be right to go to their house right now."

"What problem?"

"I don't know exactly. Something health-related."

"Serious?"

"I guess so. Yes."

"More serious than a miscarriage?"

"No, no, of course not. We could go to a hotel. Reorganize our trip from there."

Jon arranges a tray with a cup of coffee, a glass of orange juice, toast, butter and jam.

"That's not necessary. You can stay as long as you need."

Markel thanks him and promises they won't be any bother; to the contrary, they'll help however they can.

Jon brings breakfast to Katharina. She sits up in bed. He places another pillow behind her back.

"How are you doing?"

"Fine. Thanks for breakfast."

"Did you call your parents?"

She tries the coffee. No, she hasn't.

"Why not?"

"Do you want them to show up on our doorstep today?"

He doesn't bother to reply. He looks out the window. The estuary glitters. The morning sun falls full on the front of the house, like a spotlight on a stage.

"You could go to Munich. I'll go with you, if you want."

"I just said I'm fine. I'll tell my parents everything and I'll go to Munich. Later. There's something we need to take care of first. Did you eat yet? Have a piece of toast. This is too much for me."

Virginia exits a small hotel located at one end of Ribadesella's main street. She's wearing workout clothes and carrying the bag she usually takes to the gym. Sunglasses, like always. Hair in a loose braid.

From the café across the street, Katharina watches her walk briskly away, in the direction of the gym. Katharina has a table a reasonable distance from the window. In front of her, an open newspaper she hid behind when Virginia showed up. She checks her watch. Virginia was inside the hotel for twenty minutes. A three-story building, old but remodeled, with small wooden balconies. This is her third day following Virginia. The woman goes to the gym at the same time every day. Katharina leaves the house before her and hides at the end of the bridge, on the town-side, where Virginia has to pass. From there she trails her on foot, unseen. The first two days, Virginia went to the gym and then back home. But today, Katharina is in luck.

Jon orders a beer and sits at the same table from which Katharina watched the hotel. He lets a half hour pass, during which time no one enters or exits the establishment. Katharina told him that it's better for him to stay out of the hotel, in case he's recognized by the person or persons Virginia is going to see—which is the logical conclusion they've reached. They hardly slept the night before. Whispering in their room until daybreak, they speculated about what Virginia and Markel are up to. Or maybe Virginia is the only one involved. Maybe she's acting behind Markel's back.

Jon is bored after the second beer. He crosses the street and enters the hotel. Wood floors, uneven but nicely buffed. Plastic plants in large pots. A steep staircase leading to the first floor, protected by a burgundy runner. The brass bars that support the stairs are secured at the back of each step and match the handrail. The reception desk is tucked in the space under the stairs. It wasn't made with tall people in mind. Out the corner of his eye, he clocks the man behind the desk, but Jon doesn't stop, passing directly through the door leading to the dining room-bar. There's nobody. A fireplace. Nautical decorations on the walls, ship lanterns made into lamps, a display of knots. The bar, situated diagonally in a corner, is shaped like a sailing ship. It's a rough reproduction of the Habana, a vessel of yesteryear that used to cover the shipping route between Ribadesella and Cuba. The three masts—foremast, main, and mizzen—almost touch the ceiling. The sails are closed and dusty. The crow's nest serves as a shelf for the most expensive whiskeys and cognacs. The rest of the bottles sit on a shelf behind the bar. Jon takes a seat on a stool. He doesn't glance behind him when the receptionist enters the room and shuffles over. The bowsprits fold away to allow access behind the bar.

"What'll we have here . . . Holy shit! Jon!"

"Hey, how're you doing? I didn't expect you to recognize me."

"Of course I do, fuck, you haven't changed a bit," says F, hands on the bar-top, arms extended, head tilted slightly back, as if he needs some distance to focus and observe whether Jon in fact has changed or not. He shakes his head.

"Holy shit, I can't believe it."

They were at school together. Friends. F's grand-parents had owned the hotel. During the winter, when the weather was bad, they went there to play after school. The fireplace was always burning and there were always a couple of dogs dozing by the warmth from the blaze. F's grandfather was a hunting and fishing enthusiast. On many occasions, Jon had done his homework at the very bar where he now sits. Jon lost touch with F when he left Ribadesella. Turned out they weren't that close.

"You look good," he says, although F has gained weight and lost hair and is unshaven.

"Yeah, yeah . . . You, too. So, what'll it be?"

Jon points to the crow's nest. Johnnie Walker Black, with ice.

"What are you doing around here, anyway?"

"In Ribadesella?"

F taps the nail of his pointer finger on the bar.

"No. Here. You knew I took over the hotel, right?"

Jon nods. "How's business?"

"Slow this time of year. The usual. I had a few of those flying saucer nutters, but they got bored and went home or bought a tent and went out to the Prado de San Juan. Almost all our rooms are empty. But tell me what brings you here."

Jon sips his whiskey. He purses his lips, shakes his head. As if he would like to say something but can't quite get up the courage. F waits.

"The truth is, I have a problem, or think I do, and maybe you can help."

"Sure. That's what friends are for. Isn't that what they say?"

"See, I'm with this girl . . ."

"A girlfriend, you mean?"

"Yeah, my partner. At least for now. Things aren't exactly going great. I think she's seeing someone."

"Damn. I'm sorry. And how can I help with that?"

"They meet here."

"You're fucking kidding me. That stuff goes on in my hotel?"

"Her name is Virginia. Long, dark hair."

"I know who she is. One of the girls you have in your house. There are two, right?"

Jon nods. "So you've known for a while that I'm in town."

"My mother saw you the other day."

"Really? Where?"

"At the grocery store."

"I didn't see her."

"You saw her, but you didn't say hello. So, the dark-haired one is your girlfriend, eh? I was sure it was the other one. Well, the other girl has dark hair, too. The shorter one."

Jon sticks to his story. "And you said you recognize her."

"How could I not? Pretty hot. She always comes in at the same time. She booked a room and pays by the week."

"She pays for a room?"

"That's what I said."

"Does she have someone staying here? Who is it?"

"Hey, you're not going to do anything stupid, are you? I don't want any trouble. Easter week is around the corner and I've got bookings."

"Of course not. That's why I'm talking to you, so

I can find out what's going on without having to do something I'd regret."

"Yeah, of course." Again, F drums his fingertips on the bar. He's smiling. "You know what? I highly doubt the guy is involved with this Virginia character. You know, your girlfriend."

"What do you mean?"

F takes his time before answering. He's still smiling.

"How long has it been since you and I talked?" he says at last. "Hard to believe. Remember how we used to play here? My grandmother always remembered the time you got into one of the empty rooms and fell asleep. You sure caused a stir. Everyone thought you'd left without saying anything or gotten lost or something."

"All right, that's enough," Jon says, and puts two hundred euros down on the bar.

"And it's four for the whiskey," says F

Jon's phone rings. He and Katharina look at the screen. They don't pick up. They're back in the café across from the hotel. The ringing stops. It's the signal they agreed upon with F Almost immediately, a man exits the hotel. He casts an appreciative glance at the clouds and walks away.

"That's him?" Katharina asks.

"I guess so. Are you still sure about this?"

"Of course. Are you?"

Jon nods. "Be careful."

Katharina stands up. Before she leaves the café, Jon calls her name. She comes back and kisses him on the mouth.

"Mmm," she says. "See you soon."

"See you soon."

Jon watches her go after the man. Once they've both turned the corner, he leaves the café, crosses the street, and enters the hotel. F is waiting at reception. Jon lays an envelope of money on the counter; he doesn't remove his hand until F turns to the cubby behind him, gets a key, and hands it over.

"First floor. End of the hall." Hardening his tone, F adds: "Don't take anything, eh? I'm already regretting this."

Jon climbs the stairs. There's no elevator. The runner is wearing thin on the treads. Several lightbulbs are burnt out in the hall. In spite of the renovations designed to make the hotel more attractive to tourists, it still looks like what it always was: lodging for travelers passing through on business. The doors are dark wood, the room numbers are polished brass. Jon knocks before trying the key, just to make sure. Nobody answers. He glances up and down the hall, then slips inside. Silently, he closes the door behind him. They told Markel and Virginia they were going to the hospital in Oviedo for Katharina's check-up.

The room is one of the hotel's most economical. Small and dark. A narrow window looks onto the back alley. A single bed. The TV hangs from a shelf on the wall, facing the bed. Beneath it, a desk and chair. No other furnishings. On the desk: Tupperware containers of food; paper plates; a glass containing a fork, spoon, and knife; half a baguette; bottle of wine; electric kettle; packets of tea; a tin of Danish butter cookies. On the nightstand: a Spanish-English dictionary, two John le Carré paperbacks in English, and packets of pills. He examines the medication: aspirin, gastro reflux tablets, and sleeping pills. He takes a quick look in the bathroom. A rusty stain runs from the faucet down the tiling in the shower. Clothes have been hung to dry on the towel rack. On the floor under the sink: a box of laundry detergent and another of bleach. He returns to the room.

Everything is tidy, but the room's small dimensions make it look jumbled. It smells like food. There's no microwave; Jon supposes the room's occupant must eat the food cold, right out of the container, unless he has them warm it up in the hotel kitchen, something Jon doubts. Not only has F told Jon when the occupant tends to leave the hotel; he has also informed him that Virginia doesn't come every day, but every two or three. The man receives no other visitors. He hardly goes out. In the morning, while the maid makes up his room, the man sits downstairs in the bar-restaurant, where he never consumes anything.

***

The man heads for the Virgin del Guía chapel. The path departs from one end of Monte Corbero, at the base of the Atalaya Tower, ascends halfway up the mountainside, then stays level almost until the end, where a new slope climbs to the summit at the opposite end of the mountain, leading to a small hermitage. Katharina follows the man at what she considers a safe distance. According to the plan, all she has to do is tail him and warn Jon when he starts back toward the hotel. She doesn't think the man has cottoned on to her. But just in case, she makes a few stops, taking pictures on her phone like any other tourist.

The man sits down on a bench to rest midway through the climb. She keeps walking, drawing closer to him. He's older, but not old; between a father and grandfather, Katharina thinks. He's wearing corduroy pants and a wool jacket buttoned to the neck. A waxed canvas cap, the kind fishermen wear, tops his head. His clothes sag around his body, as if they'd stretched or he'd lost weight. His cheeks are flushed. His hands, folded on his lap. He contemplates the scenery. His mouth is half-open. He doesn't look threatening.

"Hola," she says in Spanish. "Do you mind if I sit here? The other benches have bird shit on them."

Though the bench has room to spare, he scoots aside and, with a brief smile, gestures for her to sit. His eyes are blue. For a moment, they both stare straight ahead, Katharina nervous all of a sudden, wondering what she's doing there, about to stand up. Before them, the rooftops, the estuary, and on the opposite bank, like red and white detail a painter would add to emphasize the greens and grays of the hillside on which it sits, Jon's parents' house. Katharina can't take her eyes off of it.

In clumsy Spanish and a heavy English accent, the man begs her pardon and asks where she's from. Her accent caught his attention, he adds.

Katharina considers whether or not it's in her interest to lie. Does this man know who she is? She doesn't have time to think. She chooses the truth. Munich. The man asks if she speaks English, and when she answers in the affirmative, he is clearly pleased. The man continues in that language. He says he very much enjoys the view. He comes up to the hermitage whenever he can. He also likes the harbor. There is a harbor in his city, but the one here smells better.

"This is a nice place," he adds. "Have you been here long?"

"A few days."

"A little longer for me. I like the town. It has a lot of history. Back there," he says, pointing over his shoulder, "on the other side of the mountain, there's a slate cliff instead of a slope, like a knife sliced the mountain in two. And at the bottom there are two caves, right beside each other. Like two eyes. They aren't natural. A warship fired two cannon balls. I don't know when . . . which wars have they had around here?"

"The Civil War . . ."

"That might have been it. The shelling created two craters and the waves have made them bigger over time, turned them into caves. I haven't seen them, of course. Though I'd like to. But I've heard about them from people I chat with when I go out."

He speaks calmly. Now and again, he wipes his nose with a white cloth handkerchief, folded but not ironed. Katharina notices a few splatters of sauce on his jacket.

"What are you doing here in Ribadesella? If you'll pardon my asking."

Katharina tells him that she's on vacation with her husband. They are traveling around Spain together.

"Ah. That's nice. Traveling with family. Do you have children?"

She smiles and shakes her head.

"I'm with my daughter. Vacation, too. And where is he, your husband?"

"He stayed back at the hotel. He ate something that didn't agree with him."

The man nods sympathetically. "Local gastronomy . . ." is all he says. "And do you like what you've seen so far?"

She sighs and smiles. More or less, she admits. She would have preferred to come in the summer, but . . . She hugs herself and mimes a shiver. She'd only been to Spain one other time, she says. As a little girl, on vacation with her parents in Mallorca. She'd always imagined the whole country was like that, bright and warm. Besides, her husband brought work along and she has to spend a lot of time on her own. She adds that things aren't turning out as she'd expected.

"So, the food upsets your husband's stomach and, on top of that, he has to work. What does he do?"

Katharina digs around in her bag and pulls out a small bag of macadamia nuts. She opens the packet and offers it to the man. Curious, he peeks into the bag, takes a nut, and pops it in his mouth.

"Mmm, thanks," he says.

"He's a scriptwriter, for television."

"What kind of shows?"

"Documentaries."

The man is surprised. He didn't know documentaries had scripts. He thought they were improvised. Or that the camera just recorded whatever was happening in front of it.

"Oh, no. They definitely have a script. It's all planned out. What do you do?" Katharina offers him the nuts again. He takes several.

"Nothing," he says. "Most of the time, I wait."

"Wait for what?"

"For my daughter, usually," he laughs. "She does a lot of exercise."

He lowers his voice and, leaning in a bit, adds that he thinks his daughter has met a guy. That's why she spends so much time out of the hotel. He hopes she'll get tired of the town, or of the guy—if he exists—and tell him that they're going somewhere else.

"My daughter doesn't like me to leave the hotel when she's not there."

"Why not?"

"I think she's afraid I'll make some sort of blunder. My knees are bad. She thinks I could fall and get hurt. Once, she surprised me when I was taking a walk around the harbor and got very angry. She likes things to be done her way. She's strict. Temperamental."

He pauses before continuing.

"I shouldn't speak badly about her. But since you don't know her, I guess it doesn't matter. Or my poor taste is less grievous, at least. I go out regardless, as you can see, and nothing bad happens to me. On the contrary, I have a chance to chat with someone as charming as yourself."

"I appreciate talking with you, too," Katharina says sincerely. She feels comfortable with this man. She resists the urge to straighten his shirt collar. He's wearing cologne or aftershave, but occasionally she detects a faint whiff of clothes in need of a good wash, perspired in and worn again.

"Maybe I'm being too serious." He studies his hands. "To answer your earlier question, I'm a lawyer. Although at my age, I hardly work anymore. Just the occasional case, usually out of obligation."

Katharina asks what sorts of cases he deals with.

"You don't want to hear about it," he says. "Dull matters. Almost always unpleasant."

On the back of the only chair in the room hangs a burgundy bathrobe with fraying cuffs. A pair of slippers stick out from under the bed. Jon opens the closet. Not much clothing, all of it good quality but very shabby. Nothing of interest. He stands on tiptoe and feels around the shelf. He touches something—a strap, a handle? He tugs and out comes a leather briefcase. He sits on the bed to examine the contents. He lays what he pulls out on the bedspread. An envelope stuffed with receipts from all kinds of establishments: boutiques, hotels, cheese shops, Duty Free . . . a date book with addresses and phone numbers, written in English with a shaky hand. An accounts ledger with lines of expenses. A notebook full of equally unintelligible memos in English. Lastly, something familiar to him: the deed to his parents' house.

This time he won't make the same mistake as when he saw the deed in the midst of Virginia's mess. He opens the window and checks out the alley. Across the way, a fishmonger's storerooms. And behind that, the rising slope of Monte Corbero. The mountain is bearing down. He waits a few seconds, spots no one. Trickles of chopped ice melt outside the storeroom. He weighs the option of sticking the documents back in the briefcase, dropping it into the alleyway, then rushing downstairs to get it. That way F would see him leaving empty-handed. But he can't risk it. Someone could use the alley in the interim. And the lane is also accessible from the hotel kitchen.

He folds the sheath containing the deed in half and tucks it in his waistband, then does the same with the notebook. He covers it all up with his sweater. He observes himself in the bathroom mirror. Hardly noticeable. The accounts ledger poses a bigger problem. It's hardbound and bulky. He tears out the last dozen pages and folds and sticks them in his pocket. He puts the datebook in the other. He returns the ledger and the envelope with the receipts—which he deems non-critical—to the briefcase and the briefcase to the shelf. He takes a last look around, then smooths the bedspread.

He leaves the key on the counter in reception.

"Did you learn what you wanted to know?" F asks.

"I learned something."

F presses his lips together. His tone has changed.

"Jon, what you've done is not okay. And I shouldn't have let you. You need to talk to your girl, not spy on her. You're only hurting yourself."

"You're right. I'll talk to her."

Jon waits a few seconds, in case F's regret spurs him to return Jon's money. Not happening.

"How long has that guy been at the hotel?"

Shaking his head, F checks the guest registration and gives Jon a date. Jon thinks back. The man arrived the same day as the dogs.

***

Katharina's phone beeps. A message. She confirms it's Jon but doesn't bother reading it. It's their signal. He's out of the hotel.

"I should go." She stands. "Keep the nuts. Please."

The man accepts them gratefully. They shake hands. He returns to his peaceful observation of the scenery, the full estuary at high tide, as if he has already forgotten Katharina. She hesitates.

"Do you want me to go with you until the hermitage? The last stretch is tough."

He waves away her offer. It's not necessary, he says. The nuts will give him energy. And besides, he adds, you need to get back to your husband. You've left him on his own long enough.

"Take good care of yourself."

"And you, my dear."

***

The next day, Virginia leaves for the gym early. She barely spends any time on the house chores now. Jon is working in the dining room. Katharina knocks on the door.

"Will it bother you if I stay in here?"

"Of course not."

Katharina doesn't have the old sweater on that she usually wears at home. She has gotten dressed and put on makeup as if she were going out. She looks out the window at the campers. Some go, others come, their number appears to remain stable.

"Do you want a coffee?" she asks.

"Sure. Please."

She goes to make it. Markel is still sleeping. A short time later, they hear Virginia come back. Jon looks at his watch.

"Would you say she wasn't gone as long as usual?"

"I don't know."

Footsteps on the stairs. Markel is finally up. A few light raps on the dining room door. He pokes his head in.

"I thought I heard you two. I'm going to town. Come with?" he asks Katharina.

She says she prefers to stay.

"Cool. Then I'll take the dogs down to the beach. They need the exercise. Need me to pick anything up?"

Katharina spends the rest of the morning with Jon. The dining room isn't the most comfortable spot in the house. The table and chairs occupy almost all the space. On the sideboard, a tray with bottles of liquor no one has touched in years. Among them, as if they were another couple of beverages, a bottle of furniture polish and a can of insecticide. She paces around the room. Gazes out the window. They speak in undertones. Speculate about how Virginia will react. Neither can quite imagine it. They ask themselves why she would be keeping her father—they're certain the man is her father—at the hotel. Just to study the deed to the house? Does she like having him nearby? Did she bring him along with her for the duration of their trip, like the dogs?

The day unfolds exactly like many of the days before. Virginia prepares lunch. Markel returns with the dogs. They eat together. Virginia seems unaware of any change.

In the evening, when they are back in the dining room, Katharina and Jon wonder if Virginia went to the hotel that morning. It's possible, too, that her father hasn't yet discovered the theft.

"Where did you stash the deed and everything else?"

"Where she can't find it. Don't worry."

Virginia has gone out for a run. They watch her come back. She sprints up the hill, soaked in sweat.

They don't get much sleep in each other's arms that night.

The next day, Virginia goes to the gym again and this time she doesn't come home. When Markel asks, Jon and Katharina pretend not to notice how long she's been gone. At lunchtime, Markel calls her phone. No answer. He tries again and again, with the same result. They hear him go into the living room downstairs. Wordlessly, Katharina and Jon follow. Jon raises the shutters and opens the windows. Katharina looks at the mess in disbelief, a hand over her nose and mouth. Markel makes his way through the chaos as if fording a swamp, kicking away wrinkled clothes and trash.

"There's a suitcase missing," he declares.

The previous night, Virginia took the dogs out for a walk after dark. She could've brought a suitcase down and hid it in the cave, Jon muses. Then, in the morning, she pretended to go to the gym as usual and took the suitcase. Maybe she called a cab and had it pick her up at the Tito Bustillo caves, that way she wouldn't have to drag the bag to the station.

"She's gone," Markel pronounces, kicking a high heel. "Bitch! How could she do this to me!" He clutches his head. "What am I going to do?"

"Markel . . ." Jon says.

"Not now!"

He shuts his eyes and takes a deep breath. Then repeats, apologetically: "Not now."

He goes into his room, where he spends the rest of the evening. They overhear him talking, pleading on Virginia's voicemail. Katharina thinks she hears him cry. Jon goes around to the garage.

"She left her dog behind, too," he says when he returns.

Markel stays in his room until nightfall. He only comes out when he hears the shouting down on the Prado de San Juan. He trudges upstairs, holding onto the railing and rubbing his face to wake up. His hair is a mess. His eyes are puffy. He steps out onto the upper balcony and joins Jon and Katharina, who are holding hands and watching the sky. The lights have returned. From the Prado de San Juan they hear the cries of shock and unbridled joy, childish cries of yearning fulfilled at long last. Forgetting their recording equipment and measuring instruments, many of the campers raise their arms to the sky.

The German Shepherds go berserk, barking madly in the garage.

They are the same three objects from before: triangular, circular, and oblong. Red, green, and blue respectively. They hover over the town, static in the sky, in triangle-formation, with the circular object at the apex. The intensity of the lights begins to rise and fall, as if the objects shared a simultaneous pulse. Each throb is accompanied by a resonant sound, sensed more in the thoracic cavity than the ears. The congregation of ufologists falls silent as the rhythm of the luminescent beat grows stronger. Markel, stunned, leans his elbows on the balcony railing. In what seems an almost involuntary gesture, he combs his hair with his fingers and tucks in his shirt.

In a strangled voice: "It's the prettiest thing I've ever seen."

The pulsing lights stop. The sound cuts out as well. Immediately, a new sequence begins. The lights on the blue and red objects shut off. Only the green—the circle—is illuminated. Expectant murmurs down on the Prado de San Juan. The green goes dark and the red lights up. Red goes dark and blue lights up. Blue goes dark and green lights up again. Like this, over and over, faster every time. And as the speed increases, so does the intensity of the light, which illuminates the whole town, the estuary, the sky. Green, blue, red, green . . . Impossible now to look at the objects directly; they've been transformed into suns. Jon and Katharina huddle together and shield their eyes. Jon has to look away. He watches the sequence of colors reflected in the front windows of the house. For an instant, he has the sense that the lights have somehow gotten inside. In a crouched position, as if bracing himself in a sandstorm, Markel perseveres in watching the objects obliquely.

It ceases. The witnesses are awestruck. The subsequent darkness feels absolute, despite the lights in town, the streetlamps, and the three unknown objects, which have recovered their initial glow. The deep, oscillating sound tolls again. In the garage, the dogs bark and strain at their chains. Markel touches his chest.

"You feel it?"

Jon and Katharina blink at him, half-blind still.

"They're addressing us." Markel displays his usual smile, enthused. "Look!"

On the Prado de San Juan, expectant silence. The odd exclamation, a hint of fear.

The circular object begins to move. It descends from its position at the apex. Parsimoniously it flies out over the town and estuary. Its shape is more appreciable. It has heft, reminiscent of a tire. It spins vertically as it glides through the air. Its rim is striated with luminous grooves. It comes toward Katharina, Jon, and Markel and flies overhead. It's wider than the house. The three of them throw back their heads, open-mouthed. The object disappears from sight over the roof. Markel runs through the house to the back door. He throws it open just in time to see the object become obscured behind the top of the hill. It is landing. The row of eucalyptus trees is silhouetted against the greenish glow.

Jon and Katharina have come out back, too. Why, they wonder, is Markel racing off down the outside stairs, toward the garage? A moment later he is back, joined by the dogs.

"It's landing! Let's go!" he shouts as he runs. "Don't just stand there!" He trips. He urges the dogs onward.

But one of the shepherds is paralyzed, tail tucked between its legs. Markel calls to it over his shoulder, but doesn't stop to wait. The other animal bolts ahead. Jon and Katharina watch them reach the eucalyptus trees and jump over the stone wall.

"I've got to go," Jon says. "That idiot doesn't even have a flashlight. He'll crack his head open."

But he doesn't move right away. He feels nauseous and dizzy. So does Katharina. They have to sit down. Jon waits a few seconds. He goes to the bathroom and wets his face. Massaging his temples, he goes to the pantry to get a flashlight.

"Be careful," Katharina says.

He finds the terrorized dog halfway up the hillside. It's Edmund, Virginia's dog, apparently unable to either advance or retreat. It whines, spins in circles, looks at the spot where Markel and the other animal disappeared. Jon keeps going. He stops at the stone wall. There is no trace of the circular object.

Behind him, the triangular and oblong forms hold their positions in the sky. There is pandemonium down on the Prado de San Juan. People have started stampeding toward the supposed landing place. The most direct route is the one Jon has taken, through his property. But the front gate is closed to the campers. They have no choice but to go around, almost a kilometer through the village of Ardines.

On the other side of the wall extends a stretch of high grass dotted with young fruit trees. The terrain then starts to slope gently toward the sinkhole. The fruit trees give way to a grove of chestnuts. Carpeted in dry leaves, the ground underfoot is springy, easier to traverse. The pulsating noise emitted by the objects hasn't stopped. Jon wishes it would. His head is throbbing. His ears hurt, like when a plane loses altitude. He makes his way around a ditch two meters wide and almost ten meters long; its edges have crumbled and the bottom is populated with ferns: an old lime kiln. The chestnuts have grown as tall as fifteen meters, close enough together for their leaves to form a tight canopy overhead; trunks covered in fungi and pale-colored lichen that forms a fringe; branches that have grown too big and broken off, supported in place by the branches of neighboring trees; dead trees, choked by brambles and vines.

"Markel!"

No answer.

"Markel!"

He has to shout at the top of his lungs. The din

is crushing. The tumult, too. Finches, sparrows, thrushes, cowbirds, crows, woodcocks, a pair of buzzards, barn owls, screech owls, all fly helter-skelter through the branches. They are joined by bats, dozens of them, hundreds. Jon ducks to take cover. He shines the beam of his flashlight upward, exposing a magpie as it crashes into a tree with a thud and drops onto the dead leaves, where it lays motionless. He turns the flashlight on the ground. Suddenly, he registers a sound he's been hearing absently in the background, eclipsed by the sonorous pulsing of the objects. Caws. Seagulls. They've abandoned their roosts and circle over the town in terrified flocks.

As much scrambling is happening on the thicket floor as in the air. Hedgehogs, foxes, polecats, weasels, wild boar, squirrels, moles, and field mice collide, tumble, continue their erratic fugue. Jon grabs onto a tree. On every rock, every stump: creepy-crawlies, frogs, salamanders, serpents.

"Markel! Markel!"

His cries have just one effect in the maelstrom that surrounds him: a single creatures stops and looks at him, ears pricked.

"Edgar," Jon says. "Edgar, come here. Where's Markel?"

The shepherd lowers its head and takes a few halting steps toward Jon. But all at once the animal appears to remember what is happening, glances up at the canopy of trees, and races off down the hill, vanishing from sight.

Jon continues to move from tree to tree. He's concerned, most of all, about the boars.

"Markel!"

It would be easy to get disoriented; Jon keeps his eyes on the ground so as not to trip over raised roots, nothing but the flashlight to guide him. But he knows the area, has points of reference—the limekiln, then another, smaller kiln, the ruins of the stone house where they stored the limestone and wood for the ovens, as well as the quicklime that was produced—that will help him find his way back. Markel does not. Jon is sure his cousin is lost. Still, he isn't too worried. Ardines is just fifteen minutes away on foot. Once Markel comes to his senses, surely he can make it there. The most probable scenario is that somebody else finds him, anyway. The ufologists will take the mountain in a matter of minutes. Jon recognizes the flashlights of the first arrivals, faint shafts of light between the trees.

These lights are quickly eclipsed by another: a green glow emanates from the dip in terrain where the sink hole is located. The circular object is lifting skyward. A crescendo of agitation in the birds and animals, perfectly visible now in the alien light seeping through the foliage. For an instant, the eyes of each and every one of creatures turn green in the glare, a pointillist abstraction. The object flies over the grove and soars in the direction of town. Desperate cries surge from area where the ufologists have started to arrive. *No! Wait! Don't leave us!*

The thicket is dark again. As if someone has turned down the volume, the shrieks and squeals settle, the scurrying stops. Jon sweeps the beam of his flashlight around him. A squirrel climbs a chestnut tree. A baby boar follows its mother into the undergrowth. A straggling toad finds shelter under a rotting trunk.

"Markel!" he says again, unconvincingly.

He is exhausted, and his fatigue quickly turns to apathy. He decides it's time to go back home.

He makes it back to the wall. The objects have disappeared. Katharina will tell him later that when the green circle rejoined the others, all three took off in the direction of the sea, just like the first time.

He picks his way down the hillside, stepping carefully. Edmund joins him, rubs up against his legs.

"Easy boy, easy. It's over. Come with me."

The dog laps his hand and wags its tail.

A welcome sense of peace comes over him. His head no longer hurts. He likes the thought of being there, at his house, with a dog. He inhales the scent of eucalyptus and fern. He tears off a leaf of lemon verbena and holds it under his nose. The smell clobbers him; it's like the leaf has been steeped in baby cologne.

Farther down the hillside, he stops to admire the lemon tree growing at the backside of the house. It's old; it was already tall when he was a boy. Some of its branches have been shored up with sticks; others, tied to the trunk with string. Always laden with fruit, abundant, sagging under its weight, a tree-shaped cornucopia.

"Stay," he tells the dog.

He goes inside. He leaves the light on outside, for when Markel returns. He tells Katharina what happened. She feels better, as well; her headache and nausea are gone. They stare out the sitting room window while sipping herbal tea. Then Jon gets some leftovers from the fridge and goes back outside. He takes the German Shepherd down to the garage and ties him up. Then he gives it the leftovers and fills its bowl with fresh water.

***

By the next morning, Markel still hasn't returned. Katharina and Jon go down to his room and search through his belongings. They don't find his wallet or passport or phone. They go into town together to do a few errands. Everyone is talking about the lights. Ribadesella and the second sighting of the UFOs are all over the media. Jon and Katharina have no interest. They stroll through the harbor. She mentions that she's going to return to translating the dentistry manual. Later that day she calls the editorial services company that hired her. Citing health problems, she says she won't finish the job by the deadline and asks for an extension, which they grant her easily. There are no complaints. No one else wants the job.

"Well," she says after lunch. "I'm going to call my parents."

She rejoins Jon after a little while. He's cleaning the downstairs living room. He's already filled three bags with trash. Katharina sits in one of the armchairs.

"What did they say? Are they coming?"

"No. I'll go to Munich."

"Me too?"

She shakes her head.

"I'll deal with reassuring them. What are we going to do with all these clothes?"

"Pack them in the suitcases."

"And then what?"

"Wait."

"For how long? Do you think she's going to come back and collect something?"

"I highly doubt it. But we'll wait a little bit. When will you go?"

"Tomorrow. My parents are getting me a ticket."

"I'll take you to the airport."

Jon spends the rest of the day putting the living room back into its original state, only taking a break to walk Edmund. He finishes putting Virginia's clothes in the suitcases. After brief consideration, he does the same with his cousin's things.

Night comes and they still have no news of Markel or his German shepherd. For some reason, the fact that the dog hasn't returned either is comforting.

Jon has tried calling Markel's phone several times. A voice recording informs him that the device is turned off or out of coverage area.

Katharina comes into the kitchen when he's making dinner. She's smiling.

"What's up?"

"My parents . . ." she says, shaking her head. "They only sent me a one-way ticket."

He keeps stirring the contents of the pot on the stove. Katharina hugs him from behind.

"Don't worry."

"I'm not worried."

Jon puts Katharina's luggage in the trunk. They hit a traffic jam on the bridge over the estuary. The town is overrun with vehicles. Several television crews have arrived. There isn't room on the Prado de San Juan for one tent more. Civil Protection and Red Cross volunteers assist the ufologists, who just keep coming and coming. As they pass the bus station, Katharina asks him to stop the car.

Seated on a bench is the man she spoke with on the hike to the hermitage. He has on the same pants and the same wool jacket. His haired is mussed and he hasn't shaved. He chews a sandwich slowly while regarding the rucksack-wearing multitude that parades before him. At his feet, a suitcase.

"Can we go?" Jon asks.

Katharina says yes.

When Jon drives by again on the way back, the bench is empty.

At home, he opens the closet in Katharina's room and checks which things she has left behind.

He sets his workspace back up in the living room. Virginia's and Markel's suitcases are stored in the basement. The weather is milder. He leaves the German shepherd loose and the door open, so the animal can come and go as it pleases. He likes working with the dog dozing at his feet. He ignores the continuing news coverage of the luminescent objects, but he can't avoid learning some information. Everyone in town is talking about it: the night of the second sighting, a death occurred on the Prado de San Juan. A woman died of a heart attack. Apparently, she was advanced in age. Jon wonders if it could be the woman with the notes. He could do a little research online, find more details or a photo, but he doesn't bother.

He is surprised by how little he thinks of his cousin. He assumes that, their plan foiled, there's nothing left for Virginia and Markel in Ribadesella and they won't be back. The memory of them—of Markel, especially—quickly fades, as it had when they'd met as children. If in fact they had ever met.

One morning he goes to the garage to feed the dog. The animal isn't inside. He whistles. It doesn't come. The front gate to the property is closed, but it could have gotten through the hedge that sections the parcel off from the road. Or who knows.

He tells himself he's waited long enough. He loads Markel and Virginia's suitcases into the car, filling the trunk, backseat, and passenger side. He drives to town. Lots of cars are still coming and going. He deposits the suitcases at a clothing donation bin. On the way back, something on the side of the road catches his eye. He stops the car. Edmund. Run-over, dead. A van brakes behind him and leans on the horn, his signal to move on.

He sits down at his computer, ready to work for a few hours straight. The house is silent. A little dusty. It's time to ask Lorena to come back. He hasn't talked to Katharina today. He's tempted to say hi via their chat, in case she's online. He doesn't do it. He's sure she'll be back soon.

9 781628 974553